IN SELDON'S HALL

In Seldon's Hall
The Assassins of Harmony: Book Five
Copyright © 2023 by Jamie McNabb
All rights reserved

Cover design by Allyson Longueira
Map design by Brandon Swann
Cover art copyright © Roberto Atzeni | Dreamstime.com

Ebook ISBN: 978-1-948447-21-8
Trade Paperback ISBN: 978-1-948447-22-5

Published by Soapbox Rising Press

In Seldon's Hall

The Assassins of Harmony: Book Five

Jamie McNabb

Soapbox Rising Press

THE METROPOLITANATE OF THE INLAND EMPIRE AND THE HOLY OREGON

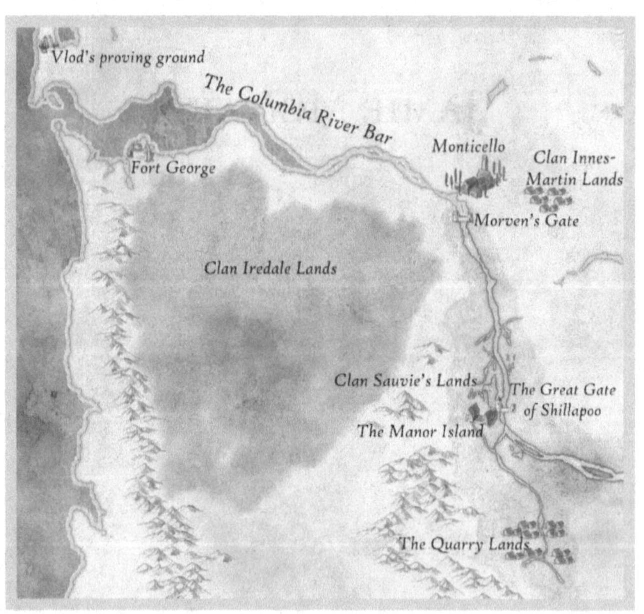

Lower Columbia River

THE METROPOLITANATE OF THE INLAND EMPIRE AND THE HOLY OREGON

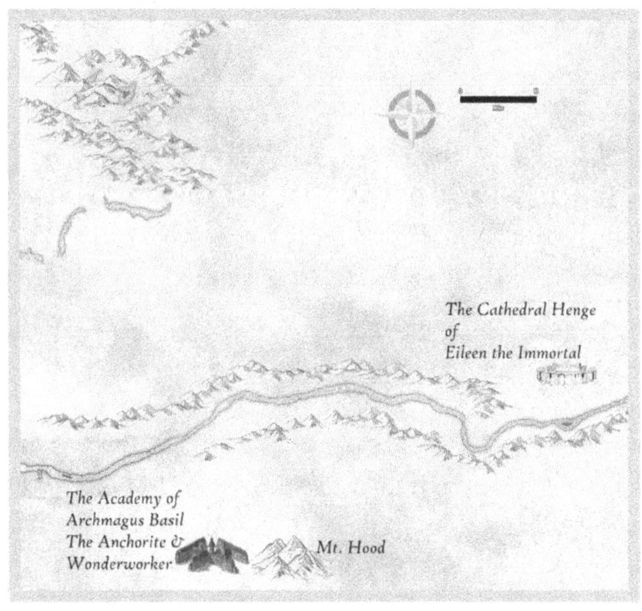

Upper Columbia River

ONE

I n the hour before the dawn, an arrow trailing white smoke signaled the turning of the tide from flood to ebb.

The hour had come to send the battle fallen on their way. They would ride the ebb to the Gods and the Generations.

Standing before the pyre, in the quickening dark that heralds the arrival of morning, Edmund, Chieftain of Clan Iredale, raised his voice and pronounced the opening salutation: "We are assembled in the Work of the Harmony!"

The congregation offered their assent to the Gods and the Generations: "Let us be so assembled!'

Apart from the anchor watches and the crews of picket boats, everyone who had been aboard the fleet had come ashore.

The congregation's voice, massed and powerful, whole and single in its nature, split the air and rolled out across the field like summer thunder. It stormed up the hillsides and echoed from the heights: "So and blessed let it be!"

At the crest of the pyre, the flags of the 7th, the 6th, the 8th, the 11th, the 4th, and the battle flag of the burned bireme billowed in the soft predawn air.

Edmund chanted "The Lament for the Battle Fallen," and the congregation, led by the mother superior of the Manor Henge of Desdemona the Shipbreaker, made the responses. Her voice was bright and clear, powerful and without a hint of strain.

When the "Lament" had been completed, Edmund; Wolfram, the Battle Master of Clan Iredale; and the commanders of the units whose flags flew atop the pyre offered prayers and intentions.

Braziers charged with live coals were set out, and unlit torches were distributed to the congregation.

An honor guard formed a wide corridor between Edmund and the foot of the pyre.

Their guide-on pennant fluttered in the freshening breeze, answered from above by the roll and rustle of the battle flags.

Edmund received the ceremonial first torch, unlit, from Wolfram's hand.

Edmund touched the torch to the glowing coals in the main ceremonial brazier.

The pitch-soaked torch caught, and within seconds its flames were issuing a column of gray-black smoke. Its aroma was like that of incense, but sharper. This was not a time of worship or celebration. It was a time of regret and grief and, paradoxically, hope.

Billowing upward, the smoke merged into the night and into the gathering dawn.

Holding his torch high, Edmund circled the base of the pyre, sanctifying the place. He strode slowly, pace by pace, holding his head up. His eyes were clear and unafraid, determined.

His torch rustled like flogging sails, but he was not in irons. His sails were trimmed and drawing.

After completing his circuit, Edmund stood before the pyre. He touched the head of his torch to the ground in the old manner.

"May we remember you!" he said, continuing with the next part of the rite. "May the Gods and the Generations of your Houses honor and welcome you! May the Harmony embrace you!"

"So and blessed let it be!"

Edmund raised his torch and threw it.

It arched high, like a missile thrown from a catapult.

It tumbled end over end, and completing its course, fell on the crest of the pyre. There, it bounced into the midst of the flags.

"May the Gods and the Generations welcome you with joy!"

The oil-drenched tinder caught.

The flames burst upward, climbing into the lightening darkness, rising into the approaching dawn.

"Victory to the Seventh! May you speak well of us!"

Edmund stepped aside, and Wolfram took his place.

"Victory!" Wolfram shouted, and threw his torch.

It landed on the second highest course of logs.

While the tinder caught and the flames took hold, Wolfram prayed silently.

Once he had finished, he turned and beckoned to the congregation in the formal manner, arms straight at his sides, palms forward, head bowed.

The congregation responded. Haltingly at first, but rapidly gaining strength, they came forward, threw their torches, and returned to their places.

Soon their fiery torches arced onto the pyre in an orange-and-yellow hail.

The timbers of the pyre caught, and the blaze danced jubilantly into the morning sky.

The Harmony claimed its own.

The Gods and the Generations embraced the battle fallen.

Their Houses would remember them!

Edmund and the whole of Clan Iredale would honor them.

While the pyre grew, while the morning and ebb took hold, the *Dirge* singers read the names of the dead into *The Dirge Common to the Manor Henge of Desdemona the Ship Breaker*, thereby assuring their immortality among the Gods and the Generations.

In due course, the names would be reported to the Cathedral, where they would be reviewed and transcribed into *The Dirge Common to the Cathedral Henge of Eileen the Immortal*. It was this rite in addition to the perpetual chanting of the *Dirge* that confirmed and assured that the dead thus remembered would have their lives in the Harmony secured for Eternity.

The *Dirge* was no liturgical formality. Rather, it was the living voice of the Gods and the Generations.

Waiting in her place among the members of her father's House, Dagna also sang the *Dirge*, but she was not singing the *Dirge* of the *Dirge* singers.

She sang her own version, privately, softly, but with confidence and transcendent intensity. She voiced each of the thirty-two melodies, and throughout each of them she chanted a single name: Zachary.

Zachary?

Who was Zachary?

It was only after Dagna had repeated the name several times that Vlod realized what Dagna was doing. She had named her dead infant and was attempting to add his name to the *Dirge*.

Involuntarily, Vlod shivered at the blasphemy.

Vlod's turn came, and he moved forward.

The wind had driven the clouds inland from the coast, and they were hanging low over the field where the Brethren had attacked, where the 7th had made its stand.

The flames from the pyre clutched upward at the undersides of the clouds, and the smoke rose as if to blacken them, as if to force them into mourning for the Iredale dead.

But the wind also pushed the clouds beyond the reach of the flames and the smoke.

"Victory to the Seventh!" Vlod called, and threw his torch.

Dagna stepped forward. So far, she had said nothing overt, nothing public. She had kept her repetition of her dead son's name private.

Well and good.

Whatever means Dagna invoked to work out her grief and her rage were her affair. She was acting on her own, in advance of the legalities. Those would be in train soon enough, and Vlod could neither blame her nor condemn her.

Stephania and Valeda had murdered the child. He had not been a weakling. In time, after the clan had rooted out and convicted the conspirators, Edmund would appeal Warrick's judgment, and the Geneticists Guild would have no choice but to act in the child's favor.

So and blessed!

In a strong voice, Dagna pronounced, "Zachary!"

"Can she ride?" Darshana asked. She was a Brethren warrior and Djarek's most-favored daughter.

"She'll need a nursemaid for the first couple of days," Yu'quiro said. Yu'quiro's hair was light brown and cropped short. She was older than Darshana but only by a few years.

"She's the midwife?"

"Yes. She's Valeda."

The midwife was barely conscious. She was looking around her, from side to side and up at the Brethren. It appeared as though she were trying to figure out what had happened to her and where she was.

Darshana had seen this before. The effects of a blow to the head and exposure were roiling together in a dangerous stew. They'd be lucky if she lasted out the day. Two days was unimaginable.

A stream of drool erupted from the corner of the old woman's mouth and coursed unheeded down her chin and dribbled onto the front of her filthy garments. She made a noise that could have been a mutter or a moan.

She'd be lucky to see sunset.

Darshana said, "We ought to let her rest awhile before we take her to the encampment."

"Your father's orders were to deliver her to him without delay."

Her father's orders... How he loved to give orders. They'd follow them, though, and when they had, they'd arrive with a corpse. He'd upbraid them for "letting" her die. Why hadn't they taken better care of the old woman. What good was a corpse? How could they have failed him in the performance of such a simple task? Were they Brethren warriors or dung-eating clansmen?

By this time, the sun had lifted, and two klicks to the north, the smoke from the clansmen's pyre was gray black against the sky's pale blue.

The sound of the clan's massed chanting was unmistakable for what it was.

Darshana studied the old woman's face.

Her eyes were watery, but they seemed to be focusing better. They were not empty. She was in no waking coma, the sort of state induced by too much alcohol, too much valerian, or too much opium. Valeda's attention darted from place to place as though she were searching for something, but she was alert enough to search, alert enough to see, to find, to reject, and to resume her search. She was whispering to herself, strings of meaningless sounds.

"She'll never survive the journey if we make her ride," Darshana said.

"That's true," Yu'quiro said.

The clansmen's chanting exploded into a sustained cheer.

"You'd better set out before they've finished," Darshana said.

They rigged a travois to one of the pack horses and strapped the midwife onto it. It was quick and crude, but it would serve.

Darshana rose onto her mount and looped the pack horse's lead around the saddle horn.

"Nursemaid to a midwife," she mumbled.

Yu'quiro scoffed. "She's no midwife."

Together, the two Brethren warriors rode off to the west, heading deeper into the buffer zone between the lands claimed by Edmund and the lands claimed by Seldon.

Bevan was excruciatingly tired, and his emotions were viciously raw, but he was back in his own apartments. He could let go for a few minutes.

His wife had intercepted him on his way in, but he'd shooed her away with the claim of having work to do that could not wait. Messages to send. Reports to answer. Wounded to provide for. He promised to tell her about the engagement as soon as he could.

Work. Reports. Wounded.

They had to be dealt with, but he had no idea of how. Time was short, and resources were scarce.

No wonder his father was the sort of man he was.

Bevan opted to tackle first things first.

He downed the glass of wine that one of the servants had brought him. The wine was cool, and it cut the paste in his mouth.

They'd brought a tray of food, but he chose to ignore it. Food would come later.

Bevan dropped into a chair and worked his boots off. They were caked with mud. It dropped onto the floor in foul-smelling clods. Dirt? Mostly it was horseshit.

How appropriate!

His wife had bought the carpet the previous summer at Seldon's. She would not be pleased.

A commotion sounded outside in the passageway.

His father's secretary was attempting to gain entrance, but Bevan's guards were refusing him.

The man's voice rose to an effete shriek.

When it came to the court's toadies, the individual outside Bevan's door stood at the top of the heap. He was spineless, groveling, insistent, incompetent, and bullying: he was Bevan's father's private secretary.

His brother, Gregory had loathed the man, and Bevan's own hatred for the creature had doubled and redoubled over the last few weeks.

Why couldn't his father have at least given him a decent chance to get out of his field clothes?

Bevan caught himself.

Like it or not, he had to shoulder what lay ahead.

Holding his wine in one hand, and with his riding cloak still draped across his shoulders, Bevan opened the door.

To the guards, he said, "Thank you. I'll take care of it."

To his father's secretary, Bevan said, "Won't it wait, Nasim?"

The man's face and body were slack with laziness and self-indulgence. His demeanor was not. It was as hard and as rigid as iron. "No, my lord, I'm afraid it won't. Your father said 'Immediately!' my lord, and I do believe he meant it."

TWO

A uniformed guard ushered Bevan into his father's sitting room. The French doors leading out onto the balcony were open. Their draperies bellied in the breeze sneaking in from the river. The breeze was pregnant with the tang of the not-so-very-distant ocean.

Pregnant.

To what, then, would it give birth?

Ships? Foreign trade? Endless war? Death and prosperity in a single package?

Given its cost, of what value was prosperity?

Bevan's father, Vernon, Chieftain of Clan Innes-Martin, was seated at his writing table. It was an enormous thing, easily the size of a meant-to-impress doorway. Its surface was scattered with papers, inkpots, files, decanters, glasses, pots, and cups.

The table faced down the length of the short room, toward the fireplace, rather than squarely toward the door. The arrangement afforded Bevan's father a view of the door, if he turned to his left, and out through the French doors if he turned to his right.

That his father didn't have his back to the fireplace was one of the man's quirks.

Near the French doors, with a pot of tea near to hand, Trevor, the battlemaster of Clan Innes-Martin, sat in virtual immobility. His face was set in an angry expression, notably around his eyes and mouth. On the other side of the coin, where Trevor's face was not angry, its expression might have been called benign or, perhaps, neutral, two hopeful signs.

Might.

Caution and experience dictated otherwise.

Bevan's absurd flight of hope collapsed.

From its niche, the vision dancer's head stared into space. Sightlessly. Had to be. She *was* dead. She could not see, well, not through those eyes. Spiritually, if the theology were to be credited, but not physically. Her eyes were two glass spheres. Glass. Inanimate. Dead. Incapable of sight, incapable of transmitting nerve signals to her brain, which was itself dead.

And yet, her eyes were unnerving Bevan. They always did. They made the muscles across his stomach tighten and caused a sweat to break out in the small of his back.

He'd heard the rumors about his father's "faithful servant," and he'd passed along a few of them himself.

Who hadn't?

Damn few.

According to one school of thought, she had revealed a vision she had danced for Bevan's father, and the instant he had learned of it, he had executed her. Personally.

To Bevan, this seemed unlikely. No dancer would ever dare to reveal a vision. He did believe, however, that for whatever reason, his father had taken her head.

Why?

Because there was the head, mounted like a bizarre trophy, a warning to those with eyes to see, with living eyes that *could* see.

According to other stories, the dancer's head could move on its own. It could smile, blink, and follow people with its eyes. There were those who claimed that it could wink. Wink!

It was said that she could chant the *Dirge*. No doubt, Bevan mused sarcastically, she could do so in a high, clear soprano, the sort of voice that caused the coldest of women to weep, the sort of voice that enthralled the most resolute of men.

The most outrageous of the tales credited her with flying about the room like a bird, or shooting killer bolts of lightning from her eyes, or accomplishing both of these feats at once.

Bevan believed none of these fantastical stories, except that his father had decapitated her. That part of the lore Bevan credited without a moment's pause. It was the *why* of it that eluded him, the *why* of it and the *why* of her display.

Wouldn't it have been better to have had it over and done with? Gone and forgotten?

Bevan thought so. Whenever he looked at the head involuntary spasms gripped his shoulders and the middle of his back. It was like a strong jolt of static electricity.

Up to this point in the interview, Bevan's father had said nothing. Indeed, he had barely looked up from what he was writing.

Prompting him, Bevan said, "You sent for me?"

"Is that a question or a statement," Vernon said.

"I'm here," Bevan said.

"You were supposed to have *raided* Edmund's fleet."

"I did."

"No, you *attacked* Edmund's fleet."

"It was a raid in force."

"Don't split hairs with me," Vernon shouted.

"As you wish," Bevan said. "If it makes you any happier, I *attacked*."

"I've had similar fits of ambition. They were expensive. How expensive was yours?"

"From your balcony you ought to be able to smell their funeral pyre."

"Don't you dare take that tone with me," Vernon said. "I won't have it!"

"Yes, my lord," Bevan said, and made his report, reciting the figures from memory as best he could.

His father listened without comment, question, or observation.

Trevor was equally closed.

It was unnerving. The both of them. Not as much as a sneer or a derisive profanity. Then again, the whole week had been unnerving, and whole year had turned any semblance of reason upside down.

Bevan finished with, "The people we needed to get ashore are ashore, and we've exercised the Brethren. From what I've seen, as mercenaries, they're worth every penny."

"They ought to be," Trevor commented. "I'm surprised you have to pay them to kill clansmen."

"It seemed fair," Bevan said.

Trevor glared at him, but didn't ask the question hanging in the room. How had Bevan come up with the money to hire the Brethren?

"What about Edmund?" Bevan's father asked.

"We have scouts watching him," Bevan said. "The best estimate is that he'll get under way with tomorrow's flood."

"Which will reach them at...?" his father asked.

"At about noon in that stretch of the river," Trevor said, answering for Bevan. "He's conserving his crews."

"I would," Vernon said. He sipped his coffee. "Review for me what happened to Stephania."

"She was captured," Bevan said, and repeated that part of his report.

"Is she alive or dead?" his father asked. "What's your best guess?"

"I'd rather not speculate."

"You ought to have found out before you left the area," Trevor said. "We'll have to assume she's alive."

"Agreed," Vernon said. "She's alive and spilling her guts. What about her father, Fahraq?"

"He's being silenced."

"By a Brethren assassin?"

"No, by one of my people."

"You don't have people!" Vernon said.

"By one of *your* people temporarily placed at my disposal," Bevan said. "One of ours."

Trevor glared anew at Bevan, but Vernon let the impudence go unanswered.

"Good," Vernon said. "Don't overuse the Brethren."

"I'd trust my life to one of them sooner than I'd trust it to one of yours."

"Oh, you poor little darling," Vernon said, and told his son and heir to get out.

Bevan may have been gone from the room, but Vernon remained at his desk. He stared out through the doors onto the balcony and tried to work his way through his son's thinking...or what passed for thinking in that quarter.

When was the little bastard going to learn?

Vernon had agreed to a raid, but his son had staged a full-scale engagement.

Further, Bevan was in danger of making a fool out of himself with the Brethren. The upriver clans were bound to notice it, and when they did, they were bound to respond. They would not sit idly by. Meaning that Narmer, the Egyptophile chieftain of Clan Pasco-Burbank, would not sit idly by.

Being the sort of rabbit-eared milquetoasts they were, apart from his pharaonic majesty, they'd whine and they'd bluster, but that would be about the end of it.

However, at Narmer's insistence and with his money jingling in their purses, when Bevan ignored their warnings and continued to use the Brethren, the upriver clans would forget their timorous ways. With Narmer in the lead, they'd swoop down through the Columbia River Gorge and dive on Clan Innes-Martin like a flock of cormorants diving on a school of smelt.

Bevan would have about as much chance as the smelt had.

But, laying out the political facts of life for his son would have to wait for a better time: when his son and heir had rested and was in a less prickly mood.

The boy had made a mistake somewhere along the line and he was consumed with his efforts to cover it up for himself and *to* himself. It was this latter behavior that was the greater disappointment.

Vernon's coffee had gone cold, and he asked Trevor to pour him a cup of tea. "Is it hot or tepid?"

Trevor sent for a fresh pot.

When they had it, Trevor poured them fresh cups of tea.

Tasting his, Vernon said, "Bloodless, colored water! Thank you, by the way. How do you stand it?"

"It's an acquired taste. It's easier on my stomach."

"I could use a touch of easier," Vernon said. He drank off a long sip and smiled. "It's hot and it's wet."

"Yes, my lord."

Vernon asked, "What do you imagine your future chieftain is up to?"

"You paid for the Brethren, didn't you?"

"Naturally," Vernon said.

"I don't like it. I'd rather sleep with a cobra."

"Plenty of those about," Vernon said.

"With any luck we'll be able to keep their numbers down."

"We'll need an army of mongooses," Vernon said. He sighed in frustration. "Enough fencing. What's my son and heir up to?"

"What are the two of you up to?" Trevor asked. "I have the outlines, but you've kept the details to yourselves."

"We're playing cat and mouse," Vernon said. "He believes I'm trying to murder him, via a legal fiction."

"Which would be?"

"Treason."

"Are you?" Trevor asked.

"Would I tell you if I were?" Vernon laughed at the bemusement and the real hurt on Trevor's face. "No," he said. "No, I'm not. Bevan will succeed me."

"Yes, my lord."

"You don't approve?"

"The succession isn't up to me. My part is to obey."

"You're underestimating yourself."

"No, my lord. At the end of the day, I either obey or I withdraw."

After a brief pause, Vernon asked, "After I'm dead, will you leave?"

"He'll want his own people around him."

"True, but he'll need you," Vernon said.

"He'll have me dead before your pyre has burned itself out."

"That is a risk."

"I won't be murdered," Trevor said.

"Let's hope we're fighting with shadows," Vernon said.

"So and blessed."

"So and blessed," Vernon repeated. Then he added, "We'll be leaving for the Feast of Mabon in a few days. I—"

The flow of Vernon's words faltered. Usually, he was able to keep his impending death out of his conscious thoughts, except at night, which was only to be expected, but with the light shining in through the French doors and the breeze bathing him, he was having trouble managing the trick.

Freeing himself from his inner turmoil, he said, "Trevor, I want you to see him safely home."

Trevor arched an eyebrow. "Do you want me to see him safely home from the feast, or do you want me to see him safely into the chieftaincy?"

"Into the chieftaincy," Vernon said. "Promise me to make an honest effort?"

"Gladly, my lord. An honest effort."

THREE

Near its top, the smoke from the Iredale funeral pyre made a gray smudge against the blue of the mid-morning sky. The wind that had been promising at the tide's turning from flood to ebb had failed, and in consequence the day itself had been left to make its own promise: to be muggy and hot.

The glare off the water made the situation worse, and Vlod's ride in the cutter out to *Koan* was tedious and wearing. The river smelled of mud and the low water that comes at the end of summer.

When the time came, a casually timed step took Vlod from the boat to the lower platform of the galley's boarding ladder. He plodded up the steps. As he passed through the bulwark, he exchanged greetings with the officer of the deck, but spoke to no one else and went below.

His mood was not anger, nor was it absorption, nor grief, nor anticipation, nor fear, nor distrust, nor preoccupation.

Reaching the foot of the companionway, he dismissed the riddle.

Maybe it was grief, after all.

Maybe it was exhaustion.

Maybe the funeral, with its fire and smoke and burning corpses, had stirred his grief for his father.

Maybe it was a question of control. Maybe the pyre had further loosened the mastery that he liked to believe he had over his grief.

Belowdecks, the galley was cool.

With most of the crew not yet returned aboard, the ship was quiet and relaxed, as though asleep, but she wasn't. With hardly any effort, Vlod made out the sounds of the officer of the deck pacing the quarterdeck, of the fire watch making his rounds, of work details here and there throughout the ship, of the hands at the cranks of the ventilation fans, and of a detail of marines sharpening their weapons.

By late afternoon, the pyre had burned down to a mound of embers, and the burial details had thrown the last of the Brethren dead into a mass grave.

At dusk, *Koan* moved into deeper water and re-anchored. A watch was set, and preparations made to get underway with the midday flood the next day.

Edmund assigned *Felicity* to transfer the ashes from the pyre downriver to the manor's mausoleum.

Wolfram objected to leaving *Felicity* on her own, but Edmund insisted. The fleet was overdue at Seldon's manor, and in any case, *Felicity* would be rejoining them there in a few days.

Wolfram, however, did not give in.

Faced with his battlemaster's opposition, Edmund agreed to assign an extra company of foot to the ship.

They also settled on Isham to take over as *Koan*'s captain. He was an older officer, but had commanded triremes and biremes for over a decade. He was good with his crews and had a reputation for steadiness in combat. He would transfer out of his current command and his executive officer would take over from him. A messenger was sent with the necessary orders.

By the time they had finished and Edmund had left the quarterdeck, where he, Wolfram, and Vlod had worked out the details, it was well after dark.

Rather than go below, Vlod stayed on deck to indulge one of his calming pleasures: watching the picket boats.

They searched between the vessels of the fleet, like wandering night spirits on the hunt. They were spectral, silent without making a show of it. Where they moved, the moon's illumination on the water blurred, only to regain clarity a few short seconds later.

Wolfram crossed the quarterdeck to join him. "Let me guess," the battlemaster said, "you're counting the patrols."

"I was about to. How'd you guess?"

"You've counted them since you were a child. Your father used to call them his 'dice.'"

"You've never told me that before," Vlod said.

Wolfram and Edmund rarely spoke of Vlod's father, but when they did, it was with affection...and purpose.

"He taught you the knack of it," the battlemaster said. "Do you remember?"

"A little." Acting on an ingrained compulsion to understand, Vlod asked, "Any idea what he meant by calling them his dice?"

Wolfram shook his head. "I asked him once, but he wouldn't give me a direct answer. Good old Badger through and through."

"Badger?" Vlod asked. He'd never heard the word used as a nickname for his father before.

"Badger. That's what we called him *before* he graduated from the Academy and became installed as Shivananda, Magus to Clan Iredale, et cetera, et cetera."

Vlod chuckled. From what he could remember, Badger seemed like an unlikely nickname. "Why Badger?"

"Because Gila Monster was too long and too unflattering," Wolfram said. "Once your father got his teeth into a problem, he'd never let go of it. He'd worry it, tease it, *badger* it until it surrendered or he did."

Badger. An example to follow, then.

Vlod asked, "What about an indirect answer, about the dice and the boats?"

A smile of recognition lit Wolfram's face. "I think he called the boats 'dice' because setting out pickets is always a gamble. We're betting they'll find the infiltrators, and the infiltrators are betting they won't. Will I make my point or not?"

"Sounds reasonable," Vlod said. "Could it be that he'd found a way to read them? Were the boats his own private Dice of Heaven? His Seven Eyes of Fate?"

"If he did, he never told anyone about it," Wolfram grinned. "You magi can be a secretive bunch!"

A run of topics opened before Vlod, but he chose to avoid them. Veering onto new ground, he asked, "What will happen to Gregory?"

"If they don't assassinate him first, you mean?"

"Yes."

"Who can say? Perhaps he'll take up trading slaves or some such money-drenched occupation."

"Not Gregory," Vlod said. "He'll find another way to spend his time."

"Sharpening his knives, like as not," Wolfram said. "I wouldn't bet on Bevan living a long and happy life."

"Neither would I," Vlod said.

Without meaning to, Vlod shifted back onto their previous ground. "I can hardly remember anything about those years, when I was little."

"That's a shame, but count it as a blessing," Wolfram said, his face hardening. "I have whole decades I'd rather not remember." He added, "Perhaps senility is a gift."

Ignoring the jest, Vlod said. "About my father, I can remember the stories, but I don't have very many memories of my own. I remember his burning: the rain and the smoke and the flames." His screams and the way his body twisted and blistered and blackened.

As if the memories themselves weren't sufficient, there was the ash from his father's execution. Vlod had transferred what he'd gathered from that miserable pouch to a ceramic urn. He kept it on an out-of-the-way bookshelf.

Wolfram shifted his weight from one foot to another, refusing to meet Vlod's gaze.

Hesitancy wasn't like Wolfram, and Vlod braced himself for what was to come, for surely it would.

And it did.

Overcoming his reluctance, Wolfram said, "Your father frightened them."

"The Mother Metropolitan and her crowd?"

"Them, too, but it was the academics who closed ranks against him." Rushing on, he said, "If there's one thing they won't tolerate, it's for one of their own to frighten them."

Vlod had a dozen things he wanted to say, but he kept silent.

Wolfram said, "Edmund sent you into the belly of the beast. If it hadn't been for Yokashima, you would have been a gone gosling." Wolfram's voice trailed off again. He'd pointed too high and had been forced to ease away. It wasn't as daring, but it was better than rounding up and having sails back winded.

As though changing subjects, Wolfram asked, "Do you remember our mother, mine and Edmund's?"

"Of course," Vlod said. It was his turn to sheet in and bear up.

"What do you remember the most?"

"The day after my father had been burned, she told me that the Gods and the Generations care about the good that we do in our lives and not about whether or not our names are sung in the *Dirge*."

"Sounds like her."

"She made me promise to believe it."

"Belief makes it true." Wolfram sighed. "It'd be wonderful if things worked that like."

"That depends on who's doing the believing, doesn't it?"

"Nicely put."

"I have my moments."

"You'd best use a few of them to remember that you scare people, too. Your stunt with the cannon filled a lot of pants."

"It was meant to."

Wolfram made a face. "How heroic of you."

"Sorry. I didn't mean to sound flippant. Best behavior. I promise."

"Good," Wolfram said. "I'd hate to lose you." He scanned the river. Turning to Vlod, he said, "Tell me, little magus, how many boats are on picket duty tonight?"

"Six, with one held in reserve in the lee of *Winter's Pride*."

Wolfram grinned. "Well done! I ought to commission you on the spot." With less effusion, Wolfram said, "May the Gods Who Watch grant those crews eyes as sharp as yours."

FOUR

Bevan sipped his evening brandy and reread the note from his agent aboard Edmund's fleet. The note was crafted in the classic style. The letters flowed one into the next, sharp and fine-edged. The words were as crisp and the script: "Stephania alive. Advise."

Crisp, indeed.

The man who had brought it, one of Yu'quiro's, was waiting in the hall outside Bevan's study room.

Had one of Trevor's people seen him? Would it be reported? Without a doubt. The real question was, would Trevor guess the full extent of the game? He might, but not without the message itself.

Bevan's stomach burned. It wasn't the brandy's fault. He was afraid.

He hated the physical sensations of fear, hated being susceptible to them; but giving in to them was out of the question.

So was ignoring them.

All too often fear was what bubbled up when the mind could not articulate its awareness of a mortal hazard.

The brave man ignores his fears and acts in spite of them, albeit with caution; but the wise man listens to his fears and seeks to discover what lies behind them *before* he acts. Only the fool plunges forward without consideration and dies.

Hoping to play the wise man, Bevan handled himself as he would an overexcited horse. He whispered calming platitudes to himself and gently drew his thoughts up. He slowed them to a sedate walk.

When it came to the raid on Monticello, attack on Edmund's fleet, and the continuing use of Brethren troops, Bevan had protected himself. His father had approved both, tacitly and explicitly, albeit not in the scope or at the level of strength that Bevan had employed. Thus, the messenger, if not the message, was safe for Bevan to own, and they were safe for him to act upon.

A spent force, or nearly so, Trevor was free to grumble as much as he pleased.

The Festival of Mabon would settle many old issues and join battle with those waiting impatiently in the wings.

Once Bevan was on the other side of the Festival, once his father had died, once the Innes-Martins had accepted Bevan as their chieftain, the rest would fall into place as easily as lovers falling into each other's arms.

But Yu'quiro's man was waiting.

Bevan reread the note. "Advise."

Stephania's immediate death would be the prudent choice, but Bevan shrank from it.

Given the amount of time that had gone by, Edmund's people would have already interrogated her, and she would have already told them everything she knew, or could reasonably guess, or could reasonably expect them to believe.

"Stephania alive."

Stephania was alive because she had answered both their questions and the ones they had not thought to ask.

But if she had, she was of no further use to them; and if she was of no further use to them, why were they keeping her alive? Why hadn't Edmund taken vengeance on her? Why wasn't she dead?

Because Edmund wanted her alive for some reason.

On that ground alone, Bevan chose to order her death.

He took out pen and paper.

But with the paper before him, and with the pen in his hand, he stayed his decision.

Why did Edmund want her alive? What did he plan to do with her?

Bevan ran through the possibilities. He sifted and he sorted, but none of the alternatives fit.

He sipped his brandy.

Until he had an answer, killing Stephania could easily prove to be less prudent than leaving her alive.

Another point weighed in on her side: alive she was a compromised asset but she remained an *asset*. Dead she was carrion.

Bevan finished his brandy, and wrote: "She lives. Report activities."

Terse. Not literature, but clear. Professional. A message to be proud of.

He folded and sealed the paper and called for Yu'quiro's messenger.

When the man had gone, Bevan poured himself a fresh brandy and carried it over to his window. The manor lights swirled around his feet and flowed like a river down to the quays. The ships and river barges were like floating cottages, huts with wooden foundations and canvas roofs. They were fireflies on the water.

How soon, he wondered, would Trevor give his father a copy of the agent's note and of his response to it? How soon would Yu'quiro's messenger be permitted to leave the manor?

No answer.

Trevor was a world unto himself, a toady with a backbone. A rare breed, that.

When the time came, he would be missed.

Speaking of time, it was time for Bevan to perform a genuinely onerous task. He'd put it off far too long, and could no longer afford the luxury of hope, not with Stephania in chains aboard Edmund's fleet.

Bevan sent for one of his own officers, Vachlar.

Vachlar was young; however, he was quick-witted, and cunning, and he did not belong to Trevor. Instead, he belonged to Bevan.

"My lord?" Vachlar asked.

"Are you acquainted with Llewellyn?"

"Yes, my lord. We've patrolled together."

"Good," Bevan said. "Llewellyn is with Clan Nehalem. You're to take a verbal message to him."

"Yes, my lord."

"Say to him, 'Fahraq dies.'"

Trevor said, "Your son's puppy Vachlar has left the manor."

To Vernon, this was not an unexpected piece of news. "Were your agents seen? Their presence guessed?"

"No, my lord."

"Has he crossed the river?"

"Yes, my lord."

"You have people following him?"

"Of course, my lord."

FIVE

T he next day, at the exact turning of the tide from ebb to flood, Vlod took the auspices. They were favorable, and Edmund gave the command for the fleet to get under way.

A strong north-northwest wind came up and strengthened, as Vlod had predicted, and within an hour, whitecaps dotted the river. The galley's rigging sang in a happy, medium-pitched tone, and the sails drew with a fine, determined will.

With the breeze on her port quarter and her bows laurelled in foam, *Koan* found her stride.

With the surgeon's *pro forma* approval, Vlod made his "magus's rounds" of the ship's wounded.

After he had washed and changed his clothes, he went to the great cabin and began his long overdue study of the trading contracts Edmund intended, or hoped, to negotiate with Seldon.

The two chieftains had spent the past six months bashing away at them, and they were in fact the reason for their having left the manor ahead of the normal schedule.

For his part, Edmund was absolutely determined that they were to be finished, augured, signed, and sacrificed before the fleet cleared for the Cathedral.

At lunch, which they ate late, Vlod, Brenna, and Edmund were permitted to enjoy Dagna's sullen, accusing presence. When Brenna made an off-hand remark about the coming year, Dagna seized upon it as an insult, throwing down her knife and fork, and stormed out.

In the afternoon, Wolfram sent Vlod his compliments and an invitation to join him on the quarterdeck.

Vlod chuckled to himself at the military formalism and went topside.

Up on deck, the galley's heel was more apparent than it was below. The starboard side outrigger was clipping the wave tops, and the rowing crews had shipped both banks of oars and tightly closed the starboard-side ports. The weather was bright and clear, and if anything, the breeze was freshening.

Pointing at a longboat and her escorting picket holding off to windward, Wolfram said, "Trevor. He's requested permission to come aboard."

An indistinct quality in the battlemaster's voice prompted Vlod to say, "He can't very well be refused."

"Edmund doesn't want to refuse him. He's below, preparing to greet him."

The picket and longboat were signaled to come alongside, and the galley spilled the wind from her sails. There was no question of heaving to in formation, let alone in the cramped confines of the river. The accommodation detail was mustered to help with the landing.

A dozen minutes later, Trevor was climbing up the leeward ladder. Stepping through the bulwark, he said, "Request permission to come aboard."

"Granted," Wolfram said, cheerfully, usurping the officer of the deck's role. "I didn't expect to see you again until the festival."

"Business." Trevor greeted Vlod, and continuing to Wolfram, he said, "Could you take me to Edmund?"

"He's waiting for you in the great cabin."

The detail was dismissed and the sails re-trimmed. The ship steadied and worked to rebuild her speed.

Wolfram led Trevor belowdecks, and Vlod fell in behind them, wondering whether Edmund had also summoned Brenna and Dagna.

Trevor was saying, "I saw a burned-out trireme on my way up. They must have hit you pretty hard."

"Hard enough," Wolfram said, and summarized the engagement, carefully exaggerating some points and judiciously understating others.

Trevor congratulated Wolfram on Edmund's newest victory, and Wolfram politely accepted. "Wasn't much of a victory, though. It was little more than a raid in force."

As they neared the door to the great cabin, Trevor commented, "They're active up north, too. They've hit the barge canals and two of the coal mines."

"Much damage?" Wolfram asked conversationally.

Trevor had offered the initial information, so Wolfram's question wasn't out of place; however, as far as Vlod was concerned, the geese would be flying south in the springtime before Wolfram received a straight answer.

Trevor said, "No, not much, oddly."

Vlod's ears perked up at Trevor's use of the word, "oddly." It was like raw meat thrown to a starving dog. But had it been poisoned?

Wolfram nodded his understanding of what Trevor had told them, but refused to follow up.

Vlod, who could afford to, deliberately took the bait. That which one was expected to believe, could be of vastly greater importance than the truth. "Odd in what way?" he asked.

"They were skirmishes, slash-and-dash *raids*, but they were *in force*, like the raid on your fleet."

"What's Vernon's opinion?"

"He's called for auguries, vision dances, spirit journeys. He has magi throwing the Seven Eyes of Fate until they can't throw the dice."

"With what results?"

"None, yet," Trevor said. "Maybe you ought to give us a hand, Vlod. You're a whole lot faster than our magi."

The barb was palpable. But why was it there? Trevor had opened the topic, he had begged to be asked, and he had signaled he had information to give them. He had invited *and* answered their questions, leaving aside whether he had lied or not. Why the barb? What was his game?

"I am no faster than they are, but it's nice of you to say," Vlod said. He let the insult founder on his pretense of accepting Trevor's words at face value and then politely setting aside their meaning.

Or it could be that Vlod was being too self-centered. It could easily be that the insult was a clumsy way of underscoring Vernon's supposed dilemma.

At a glance from Wolfram, the guard knocked on the door to the great cabin.

"Come!" Brenna answered, from inside.

The guard opened the door, and they filed into the great cabin.

In a different part of the ship, behind the locked door to his cabin, Bevan's agent read and reread his master's instruction: to leave Stephania alive.

With a stoic sigh, he threw the note into his stove. A stove in his assigned cabin, it was quite the luxury.

The paper browned, curled, and caught fire. Bevan's decision was sensible and required no genius to deduce. While Stephania was alive, Bevan had a chance of using her against Edmund, just as Edmund was planning to use her against those who had conspired to murder Dagna's baby. As yet the poor old fool had no notion of the extent of the plot against him, but no matter. He'd run it to ground...in time. If he had that amount of time. If Vernon and Bevan had anything to say about it, Edmund wouldn't.

The agent wanted to clear his mind for his next task, but as he watched the note burn, he couldn't pull his mind away from two thoughts competing for his attention. The first was that the note had reached him without incident. Its very arrival proved to him that Edmund was in violation of the Harmony. His entire style of leadership rendered him unfit to be chieftain. His self-importance and his grief threatened the entire length of the Columbia River.

The second competing thought was closer to an emotion. It was an attitude that had hardened into an axiom of the man's life. The agent hated Edmund.

The agent's hatred sprang from an instinctive revulsion for Edmund, a revulsion that the agent kept hidden from the outside.

His hatred had no cause that he could name. It arose from no bill of indictment that he could read out. It had no origin in slight or mockery or distrust.

Nevertheless, Edmund's kindnesses, such as the stove in the agent's cabin, were dismissed as cynical manipulations, and without exceptions, Edmund's slightest missteps were taken as confirmation of the agent's opinions, of the rectitude of the agent's contempt and betrayal.

Again and again, the agent had tried to reason himself out of his hatred, but his arguments had fallen upon his own deaf ears.

He prayed daily to the Gods and the Generations that They would lift the burden, but thus far, They had not.

Perhaps in time.

It was evil to kill a man for no better cause than hatred.

The agent was, however, convinced that when the time came for him to strike, his hatred would serve.

Six

Vlod, Wolfram, and Trevor did not find Edmund in the great cabin, nor was Dagna present. They found Brenna.

She told them that Edmund would be with them shortly.

Plates of cheese, fruit, and bread decorated the table.

It remained untouched and unoffered.

Relaxing, Trevor repeated the current superficial gossip making the rounds in Vernon's court.

After several minutes, Edmund joined them. His entrance changed the balance in the cabin, halting the flow of conversation and restoring Trevor's mood to what it had been when he had come aboard.

The chieftain greeted Trevor warmly, but did not apologize for having kept him waiting.

At Wolfram's urging, Trevor provided précis of the Brethren raids on Vernon's northern territories.

Edmund expressed his sympathies and offered whatever assistance might be helpful.

The decanter made the rounds, and Edmund helped himself to a slice of cheese.

Trevor set his glass on the table. His tone formal, he said, "Vernon thanks you for your expressions of sympathy for his double loss."

Edmund acknowledged the sentiment with a bow of his head.

Trevor continued, "Our grief is insufficient."

Playing his part, Edmund asked, "What would be?"

"As you yourself have asserted, my lord, despite our feelings of loss, Vernon shared your belief that the two clans are obliged by mutual advantage and the will of the Gods and the Generations to resume the process of unification."

"By what path?" Edmund asked.

"As before: by marriage."

And thus the reason for Trevor's goading revealed itself: tactical positioning. If he could throw Vlod off-balance with a barrage of insults, Vlod might react badly. If he did, Edmund was likely to dismiss Vlod's subsequent advice as biased on personal grounds, leaving Edmund that much more isolated within his own court and that much more accessible to Trevor's proposals.

Theoretically, Trevor might be able to maneuver Vlod into estranging himself from Edmund for several days or weeks, providing, of course, that Vlod could be made to lash out, if Vlod were willing to embarrass Edmund by throwing a public fit of temper. The payoff for Vernon would be enormous.

It was an interesting strategy, but it was an old and tricky one. It called for greater precision than Trevor was likely to have the finesse to deploy.

Trevor was saying, "Vernon proposes a marriage between Dagna and Bevan. Bevan's genetic health is beyond question."

Nothing was beyond question, but Vlod kept his expression as placid as a calm day on a mountain lake.

Bevan's father had opened the windows *and* the French doors, and he had pulled aside the draperies. Masses of light were streaming in, and as a result, his sitting room was glaringly bright.

His father was saying, "He won't accept my offer, not as made, but on the off chance that he does, would you be willing to marry her?"

"Would I have a choice?"

"You always have a choice."

By having a choice, Bevan surmised that his father was telling him that he could marry Dagna and be relatively secure and at peace in his chieftaincy or he could forgo the pleasures of Dagna's bed and be relatively insecure and at war off and on for the rest of life.

"Don't stare at me," his father said. "I don't care for it, and it makes you look like a landed carp just before it has its neck snapped."

Bevan wondered, did fish have necks? He supposed they did. They had to have a place where their spines and their skulls joined.

Speaking out loud, Bevan said, "I won't divorce my wife."

"No one's asked you to. Take Dagna as a second wife."

"Edmund won't agree."

"You're going in circles. Answer my fucking question!"

Bevan's mental image of Dagna contained precious little that supported the slightest notion of her agreeing to be the wife of a non-warrior chieftain.

Her physical appeal was undeniable. Physically, her beauty, like that of her sister, was ethereal *and* athletic. It promised and it challenged, it invited and it defied.

Defied?

It refused.

Bevan said, "*Your* reach exceeds *my* grasp; but, yes, I would marry her."

"Understood," his father said. He closed his eyes and pressed the tips of his fingers onto his temples. "The captain of Edmund's galley. Former captain. You've decided to keep her alive, haven't you?"

"I have."

"Good. I want her alive and thoroughly coached by the time they reach the Cathedral."

"Coached for what?" Bevan asked.

"For her testimony before the council, you dolt," his father said.

"As soon as you've worked out the specifics, I'll instruct the agent," Bevan said.

"Pull something together," his father said. "Trevor and I will review it."

Later, after Bevan had returned to his own apartments, he told his wife about his father's plans.

She took the news impassively, no recriminations and no tears. She asked, "What's your father planning for our children?"

"On paper, I'll set aside their claims in favor of the child that Dagna and I will have. In reality nothing will change. As soon as Edmund is dead, I'll set aside the child by Dagna and restore our children."

"You're underestimating her."

"If she's offered to me, I can't refuse."

"You could," his wife said. "What happened to our plans to leave the clan?"

"That was before Gregory."

"To hell with Gregory! That was before you became the heir!"

In the great cabin aboard *Koan*, Vernon's offer was out in the open. Trevor had presented it well, but no degree of diplomacy could hide the shocking rudeness of the offer's timing.

Edmund drummed his fingers on the table for a few seconds before responding. "Bevan in exchange for Gregory. It's a good proposal and welcome, but Bevan is married, isn't he?"

Trevor produced an envelope with an unadorned wax seal and gave it to Edmund. Edmund broke the seal and read.

Without commenting, he refolded it and handed it to Brenna.

Following his signaled intention, she put the letter in a dispatch box on a sideboard, without so much as glancing at it.

Edmund said, "Bevan is married. He has a son."

"For the sake of the two clans, Bevan has agreed in principle to take a second wife and to set aside his current children," Trevor said.

"I'm aware of the Council's rulings," Edmund said. "As I stated, Bevan has a son. What about the succession?"

"A new protocol of succession can be enacted," Trevor said. "It is, my lord, a trivial matter."

"I'd rather you didn't presume to lecture me on what is or is not trivial."

"My apologies, my lord," Trevor said. "I meant no disrespect."

"Of course not," Edmund said, and rolled his signet around his ring finger. "Trivial to whom? Not to the displaced son once he's figured out what we've done to him."

The gesture with the ring was a private signal within Edmund's household; a rolled signet was a request for Vlod to intervene in a discussion. To Vlod, the next question was obvious. "Will Bevan's wife consider it be a trivial matter?" he asked. "How long before she has Dagna...out of the way?"

"She's loyal to Bevan and to her clan," Trevor said.

"She'll do as she's told?" Brenna asked.

"If you like," Trevor responded.

"What a hopelessly stupid bastard you are," Brenna said, quite kindly.

Edmund and Wolfram kept their faces stony. Two could play Trevor's throw-'em-off-balance game.

Trevor said, "She is—"

Vlod didn't give him a chance to get his feet under him. "Brenna may be overstating the case," Vlod said, matter-of-factly. He worked the stem of his wine glass between his thumb and index finger. "Tell me, what sort of a woman is she? In private, where it counts. Is she generous or small-minded?"

"She's the sort of woman who understands necessity," Trevor said, his words a shade too abrupt.

"She's a generous woman, then."

"I've found her to be so."

"Is she generous enough to damn her own children in an attempt to secure the fortunes of those of a rival?"

"If needs be," Trevor said.

"Alas, I must demur," Vlod said. "I would weep if a woman of that sort were the mother of my children."

Trevor's face reddened in anger, but Vlod continued to smile, his face relaxed, radiating tranquility.

Edmund asked, "Will you be travelling with us to the Great Henge or will you disembark at Seldon's?"

It was a fair question. Marriages between the children of chieftains weren't to be negotiated in an hour or two.

"Vernon had hoped for a swift answer," Trevor said. "His proposal is virtually identical to the arrangement between Dagna and Gregory."

"The groom is new."

Vernon closed the file on his desk. "Mark!" he bellowed at the door, surprised that he could produce a credible bellow.

The door flew open and Mark rushed into the room. "My lord?"

"Tell the stables that we're going hunting."

"Yes, my lord. For how many horses shall I ask?"

"Two. Hunters. One for you, one for me. Fast, jumpers, willing to run, a healthy lust for blood, and a touch of a mean streak!"

"Yes, my lord."

"I'm drawing a blank on names, but I must have several horses that fit that description. Don't let the stable fob off a couple of dray horses or cavalry types onto us. They've tried that stunt before and I won't have it! I will not have it!"

When Mark didn't move, Vernon said, "Get! I'll be along."

He listened to Mark's boots thumping down the corridor outside. The young man had intelligence and bravery. His devotion was embarrassingly overdrawn, but devotion was no bad thing.

When the passage was silent, Vernon went through to his dressing room and changed into hunting clothes.

The odds were better than even that out of concern for him, Mark would find horses that would turn out to be too gentle, their souls too placid, their characters too domesticated. In the end, doubtless, he would have to select the horses himself.

He finished dressing and went down to the stables, running names through his mind.

Mark met him in the yard.

He was leading Sasha and Stavros!

Of course! They were two of the manor's more notorious and feared hunters. They could run from one day into the next; they were wild, broken to the saddle, eager for the hunt, but untamed. They were as near to insane as made no difference.

They were the very embodiments of the type of horse for which he had asked. They were the horses for which he would have asked by name had the morning not sent his wits into a black muddle!

Sasha and Stavros!

Stamping, pawing, rebellious ecstasy!

Vernon was happy to admit that he had been wrong about Mark. The boy was no fool.

Such horses!

———

When Trevor had left the great cabin, Brenna said, "An immediate answer? They're trying to panic us into an agreement."

"My thoughts," Wolfram said.

"Not mine," Edmund said. "Vernon is pressing us because he sees no reason for delay."

"Can he be that ignorant of his own son?" she asked.

"Problems simplify to a man who's dying," Edmund said.

"What was in the letter?" Brenna asked.

"He says that he intends to offer himself at the Cathedral."

"Good for him. I would in his place," Wolfram said. "It'll put Bevan into the chieftaincy immediately. From there, he'll be unassailable in the short run, assuming that Vernon has already concluded an alliance with us."

"I agree," Edmund said. "Time is against Vernon, and it's against Bevan. He'll have to prove himself out of the gate, or Narmer will gobble up the leftovers."

Time was also Edmund's enemy: an aging fleet, festering resentments, an uncertain succession, and Narmer's burgeoning ambitions. If it hadn't been for Vlod's cannon...

Brenna said, "Time must be terribly different for Vernon. It is for the year kings, when the sun is tracking north instead of south."

"I dare say it races forward," Edmund said. "What was important, isn't. What wasn't important, is."

"Worse," Wolfram said. "You can't do it tomorrow because you don't have a tomorrow."

"I barely have the rest of today," Edmund said, trying to make a joke.

Vlod finished his wine. "As I see it, you can't reject the offer and—"

"You can't mean for us to accept," Wolfram said.

"—and you can't accept it, either."

"What?" It was Edmund's turn to demand an explanation. "I can't reject the offer and I can't accept it? What do I tell Trevor?"

"A non-result will have to serve," Vlod said. "Dagna is to remain in seclusion for the next year. At the end of that time, negotiations will resume."

"Narmer won't wait a year," Edmund said, "and Vernon doesn't have a year."

"Neither, my lord, does Bevan."

Dagna finished her letter to Gregory and sealed it with blue wax and a monogrammed seal. She blew on the hot wax to cool it.

They had refused to allow Gregory to see her before they'd returned him to his father, and since that morning, line by line, in the privacy of her own thoughts, she had composed her letter. But when she had set herself to take a pen into her hand and write it out, the words would not go onto the paper as she had composed them. Their passion had waned, and her sentences realized themselves as vapid strings of platitudes, void of both love and backbone. She had had everything to say to him, her love to express, vows that she had wished to make to him, but what she had ended in putting down was little more than an exercise in self-indulgent sentimentality, no matter whether it was one of love or hate.

But it had gone down, and she would not retreat from it. If her skills were inadequate to the task she had assigned them, so be it. The letter was his and she would send it to him.

She hid the neatly folded and sealed packet at the bottom of her clothes chest. At Seldon's or at the Cathedral, it made no difference which, she would find a way to have it delivered to him.

Trevor reacted with anger and indignation, both of which he attempted to conceal beneath his request for permission to leave the fleet. He smiled repeatedly, and waved convivially as his boat cast off.

Several minutes later, Vlod watched from the quarterdeck as Trevor raced toward the river's eastern bank, where, no doubt, an escort and fresh horses were waiting for him.

The answer that Edmund had given to Trevor was his, but the reasoning behind it was Vlod's, and Trevor, let alone Vernon, was less of a fool than most. He was bound to see right through the rhetoric and respond accordingly.

So and blessed.

Brenna came up and stood next to him. "Walk with me," she said.

They went forward.

When they were in the shadow of the forward catapult, she asked, "You're an augur. Your auguries haven't been worth shit lately. Have you gone blind?"

It wasn't as though he hadn't asked himself the same question dozens of times. "Most auguries aren't worth shit."

"Answer the fucking question or go live in a cave."

"All right. I may have. I may be blind."

"Find out!"

"I fully intend to, but it will have to wait until we reach Seldon's."

"Fine, but not one minute longer."

SEVEN

Edmund's fleet reached Seldon's downstream marker at sunset.

The marker was a basalt tower surmounted by three vertical red lights. These lights were paired with a similar display on a buoy moored to the northeast in the middle of the main channel.

Recognition signals were exchanged with Seldon's river command, who garrisoned the tower and guarded the water-born approaches to his manor. The river command also provided pilotage and customs services.

Koan moved from the center of the fleet to its head and took over direct communications.

After the obligatory salutes, the river command sent:

ALL ELEMENTS DISPLAY RECOGNITION SIGNAL T V X STOP
REPEAT T V X STOP
STANDBY TO RECEIVE PILOT STOP
UTMOST CAUTION STOP
DREDGE WORKING STOP
WELCOME STOP END IT

"Talkative, aren't they?" Wolfram said.

The galley repeated the message back to them and added:

UNDERSTOOD STOP END IT.

Clear codes were exchanged, and the units of the fleet instructed.

The TANGO, VICTOR, and X-RAY flags broke from *Koan*'s signal yard, and Wolfram slowed the fleet and doubled the forward lookouts.

The river command's pilot, an odious hulk of a man, came aboard and collected his fee. With the coins in his money pouch, he went to the starboard side of the quarterdeck and embarked upon a stream of useless chatter interspersed with grunts, guffaws, and profanities.

The evening hardened into night.

The northern tip of the Manor Island came broad onto the starboard beam.

Off to port, on the far side of the river, beyond the fleet, a river barge was entering the mouth of the Lewis River. The Lewis was one of the five rivers of which Vernon was lord.

Of greater geographic significance, the Lewis provided drainage for the Three Lakes, also Vernon's, irrigation for his farms, and races for his mills.

After decades of neglect, recent dredging had reopened the navigation channel, but the Lewis, judging by the care with which the barge was being handled, had lost none of its notoriety for mud and sand.

The barge was riding low, her sails doused, proceeding under oars alone.

Vlod opened one of the telescopes kept on the quarterdeck and trained it on the barge. A leadsmen was in the forward chains, portside, with another to starboard. The barge was carrying no deck cargo, but she had a large crew about.

Aft, the captain was pacing from rail to rail, his hands clasped rigidly behind his back: A man of naval training, then. Not a casual hire.

Given the way he was hunching his shoulders, he did not appear to be happy with his lot. Edmund's fleet was on his quarter and the Lewis was under his bows. Riding low, the barge's oars were making barely fifteen strokes a minute. Vlod re-counted: nearer on to twelve. He was a cautious man, untrusting. No buoy or range would have the charm needed to seduce him. What bitter experience lurked behind such feverish timidity?

Wolfram snapped his glass shut. "What do you make of her, Vlod? One of Seldon's or one of Vernon's?"

It was a matter of curiosity, for the barge's ownership was beside the point. "What's her cargo, and how many of her would there be if we weren't here?" Vlod asked.

"What'll she be hauling outbound?" Wolfram asked, stating the question. He spoke quietly to the officer of deck, who nodded and hurried below. "Not dredge tailings."

"No, not dredge tailings," the executive officer agreed.

Minutes later, the galley's cutter dropped astern and swung onto an easterly course, unnoticed by Seldon's pilot, who was definitely the sort of fool who would have raised a ruckus had he seen.

Following the curve of the river, the fleet's course bore southerly. Several klicks ahead and a few degrees off the starboard bow, the undersides of the lowering clouds glowed a dull yellow orange. By looking slightly away from it, Vlod could make out the columns of smoke rising from Seldon's furnaces and forges.

Following Vlod's gaze, Wolfram asked ironically, "I wonder what's got them working into the night?"

Vlod checked the quarterdeck before answering. The pilot had moved to the port side, out of hearing. "Customers," Vlod said, his voice as soft as he could make it. The breeze had fallen off and shifted to the south. It was warm and sluggish, heavily laden with the odors of wealth and the manufacturing of death. "Customers with cash."

Vernon listened to Trevor's report without comment. The torches lining the garden walks made a soft rustling sound, like a draft playing with sheets of paper on a desk. The garden was a simple place, a place of beauty no matter the time of year. Geometric paths, flower beds that flowed around artistically placed boulders and trees. Patches of lawn. A fountain. Benches.

Beneath the idyll was an unrelenting struggle, an endless parade of agony and death. Birds feeding on insects and spiders, insects and spiders feeding on one another, insects feeding on plants, plants crowding out one another for soil and sun. The odd snake. The odd mole.

When Vernon looked at the garden, he perceived beauty; when the dwellers in his garden looked upon one another, they perceived those they might eat and those that might eat them.

Vernon put them out of his mind. The air was pleasant, and the night was warm.

He sat on a bench and permitted Trevor to drone on for several minutes before sending him away.

Of course, Edmund was delaying. He had too many questions not to delay. Of course, he suspected Bevan. He'd have to be a fool not to. Of course, he suspected Vernon's motives. He'd have to be senile not to.

Trevor, old friend, use your head! See the patterns! Lay the groundwork for what must come next.

Vernon sat as quietly as he could, smoothing out his thoughts, permitting them to run through channels of their own making, commanding his inner voice to silence. He would not interfere with them. He would not take their freedom away from them. Too few things were free, and, for the present, he had the power to free his thoughts and so he did.

His eyes closed and he took in the aroma of the garden. He listened to the fluttering of the torches, to the violent rustling in the bushes off to his right.

A hand touched his arm and he looked up. Mark was standing over him.

"My lord?" the boy said.

Vernon gathered his thoughts from their scattered journeys. He cleared his mind. "What is it?"

"You ought to be inside."

This was too much! The child was patronizing him, but Vernon couldn't bring himself to be disgruntled. "I ought to be wherever I am," Vernon said, by way of reasserting his authority. If he gave in to them, they'd coddle him for the whole of the distance to the Mother Metropolitan's knife! "I ought to be wherever I choose to be."

"Yes, my lord."

The Inland Empire and the Holy Oregon had one too many magi. The time had come to thin the herd and be done with it.

"Pull my son's head out of his ass and bring him to me. Oh, and wash his face before he gets here."

Living up to the tower's warnings, the traffic on the river was anything but sparse. The navigation lights of commercial and military vessels dotted the channel ahead. In addition, at intervals, the galley passed groups of fishing boats, ablaze with torches, working in the shallows. Campfires punctuated the shoreline on both sides of the river.

Two klicks upstream from the tower, they left the Barbican Island Junction Buoy close aboard on the starboard beam. The buoy marked the place where the Holbrook Channel flowed into the Columbia River. The Holbrook Channel was a narrow flow of water that divided the Manor Island, as the core of Seldon's lands were formally called, from the bottom country and the range of hills to the west.

The Barbican Island itself was a fortified mound of sand that protected the northern end of the Manor Island proper and, in the military sense, commanded the downstream approach to it.

Over the centuries, the successive holders of the Manor Island had fortified and refortified Barbican Island. In addition, they had connected it to the main island with an equally fortified causeway.

The causeway dated from the time of Milton the Gaunt. Rumor had it that a brick-lined tunnel ran beneath the channel and parallel to the causeway. The question of why anyone would undertake to construct such a patent deathtrap remained unanswered.

As the galley brought Barbican Island onto her beam, Wolfram gestured dismissively at its walls, battlements, and towers. They ranged rank upon rank, higher and higher, in an apparent effort to subdue any would-be attacker by simply looming over them.

Wolfram pronounced judgment. "Overdone," Wolfram said, as he did every year. "Ought to be razed and the rock put to better use."

Two of Seldon's fast pickets arrived from upriver. They set themselves to darting in and out between Edmund's ships. The fleet's own patrols shadowed them, and the formation took on the look of a plodding bear being harassed by a swarm of drunken fireflies.

Wolfram said, "Captain, *Gorge Dancer* is off her station. Signal her captain to mind his ship, or I'll have his hide for chafing gear."

And his guts for fiddle strings! Vlod thought.

The message was sent, and *Gorge Dancer* acknowledged.

Mugs of coffee appeared from below.

By rights, Vlod ought to have gone to bed, but he lingered on deck. A ship at night was a rare joy, and he was determined to take full advantage of the opportunity.

The coffee was strong and hot. Vlod held the cup in both hands and leaned against the railing. Above him, the catapult branched upward, reaching toward the starless sky like the horns of a nightmarish stag.

What a miserable summer they had had: cold, wet, fog, and clouds. It had been a succession of gray, miserable days that had strung themselves out through July and August as though no end to them were possible, and, not surprisingly, no end had come.

There had been warm days, a stretch of them here and there, but on the whole...

The one expected change had been that from the latter part of June on, the hours of daylight had grown shorter and shorter.

Vlod longed for the dry heat of an honest summer or for the cutting cold of a winter storm. He knew the sort of weather he wanted deep down: the driving fury of a gale that would purge the ocean of shipping, a black-hearted bitch that would send the traffic running for shelter, a widow-maker with deafening winds and rank after rank of waves the size of mountains.

He knew what he would do with it. He'd take out his father's cutter. He'd triple-reef the cutter's main, double-reef and set the staysail, and cross the bar outward bound. With the lightship on his quarter, he'd flip of a coin. Heads he'd turn south, tails he'd turn north, and if it fell overboard, he'd bear off to the west.

His father had loved storms, and it had been too long, too long by half, since Vlod had gone offshore to sport with a gale. Pay off and run! Bend on the winter canvas, buckle on a harness, and go!

A signal light flashed on the eastern side of the fleet.

FLAG BYBEE'S PRIDE STOP

"Answer the call," the executive officer ordered.

The lamp clattered out an acknowledgement of the call.

Bybee's Pride sent:

FLAG BYBEE'S PRIDE NEAR REPEAT NEAR COLLISION WITH
SELDON'S PICKET FALCON'S CLAWS STOP
NO REPEAT NO DAMAGE STOP
REQUEST INSTRUCTIONS STOP END IT

Referring to the captain of *Bybee's Pride*, Wolfram said, "He's gathering the splinters for firewood."

After ordering *Bybee's Pride* to stand by for new maneuvering instructions to the fleet, Wolfram ordered the ships slowed and the fore-and-aft intervals opened.

When the fleet had acknowledged the instructions and had signaled their readiness to comply, the EXECUTE command was given.

From across the water, Vlod could hear the officers in command of the neighboring ships calling out the necessary orders to their crews.

Within a few minutes, the fleet had doubled its length and slowed until it was making barely one klick per hour over the ground.

The pilot objected. They were in a deep, well-marked channel. Edmund's fleet had no reason not to make better progress.

"Then call off your terriers," Wolfram said. "Trust me, we can stay out here all night long."

"I'm your assigned pilot. Your fleet is under—"

Wolfram laid his hand gently on the pilot's shoulder. "This is Edmund's fleet, and it's under Edmund's control, not yours." He gave that a few seconds to penetrate. "My advice? Shut your mouth, do your job, or leave the quarterdeck."

The pilot made noises about the entrance into the inner harbor, but he drew away.

Brenna came up onto the quarterdeck.

She stood next to Vlod in his chosen out-of-the-way corner. She held her gray field mantle wrapped tightly around her shoulders, as though an unnatural chill had entered the air.

Her voice pitched not to carry, she asked, "Will you have a chat with Tremayne?"

"About those auguries?"

"No, about the weather, you dolt."

Tremayne was one of the junior magi attached to Seldon's court.

The son of a Stockholm-tar manufacturer, Tremayne had grown up on Iredale lands, in Fort George, the Iredale capitol. He was a few years older than Vlod, Brenna, and Dagna. He had treated them, alternatively, as charges for whom he was responsible, as equals, and as tiresome annoyances.

As a magus, he was without equal on questions of prescience, augury, and the arcana of technique. Whether Seldon's senior magi recognized his talents was *not* open to question. They didn't.

"I might," Vlod said. "It would have to fall right."

"Don't be too picky about it," Brenna said.

"No, of course not."

"Don't shout it from the rooftops, either."

"I wasn't planning on it. Any other suggestions, your imperiousness?"

"Don't get cute!" she said, her voice growing loud.

"Then don't treat me like an imbecile!"

"Pipe down, you two," Wolfram growled at them.

"Yes, sir!" they answered in unison, sounding a feeling of eight or nine years old.

The moved aft to the taffrail.

Brenna asked, "How far are we from the manor proper? We must be close. I can smell the stench."

"Stench? That's the aroma of money being made."

"Seldon's money," Brenna commented.

"Would you deny him the fruits of his labor?"

EIGHT

Twelve klicks and twelve hours later, *Koan* and the fleet entered the Knapp Point Channel.

Off the galley's starboard bow, the towers flanking the entrance to Seldon's inner harbor rose above the walls like the bodiless legs of a mythic giant. Above the towers, the red-and-black flag of Seldon's House fluttered in the breeze. Meanwhile, the unit flags of Seldon's army flew along the crenelated bridge that connected the towers.

Edmund said, "Hoist the Iredale standard!"

When it broke from the top of the foremast, with Edmund's personal flag streaming from the signal yard, the order was given, and the galley moved to the head of the formation.

Leading the fleet, she rounded the Lower Jetty. The Lower Jetty had a twin a hundred meters farther upstream. The stretch between them formed a staging and temporary-mooring area, the so-called Outer Harbor. The term was a blatant exaggeration.

Regardless of what it was called, it and a goodly portion of the Knapp Point Channel were searched by throwing engines mounted along the walls, the connecting bridge, and atop the towers.

Koan halted smartly before the gate to the Inner Harbor. This gate was a grandiose construction called the Great Gate of Shillapoo. Its bronze-shod doors were dazzling in the morning sun.

The doors were closed.

"Hoist the gate flag," Edmund commanded.

Seconds later, the gate flag—a yellow square with a white circle in its center—broke from the signal yard.

The gate remained closed.

"You have to dip," the pilot said.

"Since when?" Edmund asked.

"Last year, my lord."

Edmund arched an eyebrow. "You have to be joking."

"No dip, no gate," the pilot said smugly.

"I'm sure my brother Seldon has his reasons," Edmund said.

"I wouldn't know, my lord," the pilot said. "I don't make the regulations."

"Very well, by the book," Wolfram said, and ordered the dipping of the gate flag.

Banners displaying the rose-and-trident emblem of Seldon's House hung down the face of the towers flanking the doors, while Seldon's personal flag flew from the top of the gate's signal mast: the chieftain of Clan Sauvie was in residence.

No answer from the gate, and the doors showed no sign of opening.

"I'm glad he's home, but I have a fleet to moor," Wolfram said. "Use semaphore. Repeat our request to enter the inner harbor."

A tedious stretch of two-way flag chatter ensued.

Time passed, as trumped-up followed trumped-up delay.

In the end, Seldon's harbormaster held the first arrivals in the outer harbor until the balance of the fleet was hove-to in the center of the channel.

Only then, with the entire fleet stationary under Seldon's catapults and trebuchets, was the harbor master willing to be satisfied that all was in good order, that the pilot hadn't been kidnapped and tortured, that the Iredale's were willing and able to pay the applicable mooring fees, that the fleet was free of plague, and that Edmund wasn't planning a sneak attack.

It was only after the harbor master had been persuaded on all these points that the outer crossbar swung from the horizontal to the vertical, that locking rods withdrew, and that the doors swung slowly outward.

The Manor Island's belief in the military invincibility of the Great Gate of Shillapoo had a long history of encouragement. Indeed, that belief had constituted an integral feature of the gate from its very inception by Shillapoo the Younger.

Shillapoo the Younger had been the grandson of Shillapoo the Great and a direct, though distant, descendant of Shillapoo I and his wife, Eileen the Immortal, to whom the regional Cathedral henge had been dedicated and for whom it was named.

Among Shillapoo the Younger's appellations were Victor of the Oregon, Fearless Bane of the Brethren, Defender of the Cathedral, and Wise Benefactor of the Magi.

It was also claimed, though less publicly and despite a distinct lack of supporting evidence, that he had invented the sailing river barge, in its present form, together with gaslight fueled by cesspit methane, the dry dock, and the compound crossbow. He was also said to have been responsible for the reintroduction of rudders on large vessels, as opposed to steering oars.

In just the same way that much was claimed on behalf of Shillapoo the Younger, so, too, much was claimed, and encouraged to be claimed, on behalf of his gate.

The engineers who had designed it and the builders who had built it had assured their client and his court that with the locking rods in place, the doors alone were easily strong enough to withstand the ram of a war galley hurled against them at flank speed.

Further, they asserted that in order to force the doors open by ramming—when the crossbar and the rods were in place—it would be necessary to shatter the doors, their framings, and the additional structures surrounding them. The accomplishment of such a task, they assured Shillapoo the Younger, would be inconceivably difficult.

Demolishing the doors by sapping or demolition, they said, was a feat that lay beyond the reach of the bravest sappers and the most talented siege masters.

Hurrah!

So they said, and so Shillapoo the Younger agreed. He had worked out the figures for himself. He had built models, and he had studied them closely.

Money changed hands, and the final drawings were approved.

The appropriate sacrifices were made, the ground was broken, and the cornerstone was laid—with the Year King for that year sealed inside of it.

As construction proceeded and the inevitable difficulties were overcome, the Willow Gate, as it was then called, deeply impressed many of the members of Shillapoo's court. His brother-in-law observed, "The Willow Gate is a brilliant achievement of talent, engineering skill, manorial-leadership genius, and our chieftain's unwavering steadfastness. The gate and its construction will stand throughout the ages as a guiding beacon and unforgettable exemplar of what is possible for people to achieve with inspired leadership. I weep for the generations of the future, for those not yet born. I weep for them because they are not alive in these glorious days, not alive to witness the rule and beneficence of Shillapoo the Younger!"

The military members of Shillapoo's court were also deeply impressed. For example, Shillapoo's battlemaster, Buckmire the Bald, was reported to have observed, although he did so very privately, "Only an idiot would throw away his resources on building that damned gate."

On the advice of his mistress, Penelope the Weaver, Buckmire the Bald hastily revised his sage comment to "No attacker would be so idiotic as to waste his time, galleys, or troops in an assault on the Willow Gate and its associated defenses."

But it was too late! No sooner had the revised statement made the rounds, side by side with its original, than Shillapoo the Younger had called his battlemaster into his presence.

It is said that Shillapoo the Younger personally and patiently explained the military and political significance of the Willow Gate to his battlemaster.

The statement was then re-re-edited by Buckmire the Bald—under Shillapoo's generous and patient tutelage—to read, "The Willow Gate is the inspired vanguard of our heroic and invincible manorial defenses!"

And thus it had remained.

And thus in solemn council assembled, Shillapoo's clan, acting on his brother-in-law's motion, as seconded by Buckmire the Bald, had elected to change the name of the gate from "The Willow Gate" to "The Great Gate of Shillapoo."

And thus it, too, had remained.

In unalloyed fairness, the gate's reputation was not entirely without honest merit. The curtain wall flanking the gate, that is, the reinforced section overlooking the Outer Harbor, was hung with the rams and decorative sternposts of the many war galleys that had, over the decades, sought to disprove the gate's reputation for invincibility. Among these trophies were two entire hulls. One bore a shattered ram and the stumps of her two masts, while the other was complete with her oars and the skeletal remains of her captain, still lashed to her tiller.

Wolfram gestured at the tiered battlements, towers, and doors, at the crenellations and arrow loops. "The whole damned thing invariably reminds me of a layer cake. I half expect a dancer to come jumping out of it."

When the doors had been completely opened, the harbor master gave the signal, and the portcullis was raised. When it was fully retracted into its housing in the lintel, in the massive bridge that connected the two towers, a horn sounded, and vessel by vessel, Edmund's fleet was graciously permitted to pass into the Inner Harbor.

The pilot directed *Koan* to a mooring buoy on the deep-water side of the basin, but Edmund countermanded the order and instructed the ship's captain to drop the hook within bowshot of the quay below Gilbert Hall, Seldon's personal residence and the seat of his government.

Vlod chuckled to himself at the pilot's spluttering and at the indignant fit of signaling that broke out from the harbor master.

After all these years, one would think that Seldon's people would know better than to attempt to dictate to Edmund.

Two hours later, with the last of the units heading for their assigned moorings, Wolfram ordered, "Signal, 'ALL CAPTAINS'!"

"'ALL CAPTAINS,' aye aye."

Edmund smiled his approval. "I'll be damned if they'll moor wherever Seldon tells them to."

Seldon may own the island, and the harbor with it, Vlod thought, but Edmund owns his fleet. And because Vlod's lord did, he automatically took possession of the waters through which his ships sailed, the docks and piers to which they tied, the mooring buoys they picked up, the anchorages in which they dropped their anchors, and the mud that clung to the flukes of those anchors.

But "The magi do not have lords!" a remembered voice cautioned Vlod. "You will *serve* the chieftains to whom we assign you, but you will not *obey* them. They may not command you, and you may not follow their commands. It may appear that your do, the language is much the same, but, hear this now, you do not."

Questions and explanations—the practical differences between orders and requests, for example—had followed.

Then, finishing the lesson, the remembered voice had pronounced, "Oaths of fealty are unknown between magi and those who are not magi."

Koan reversed her oars and slowed to a stop.

"The magi do not have lords," the voice repeated.

The rowers rested. They held the blades of their oars clear of the water.

The directive had been solid enough when issued from a podium in a classroom at the Academy, but in the outside world, in the court of a major chieftain, the circumstances of a magus's life rarely conformed to the delineations dictated by an academic or by regulatory theory. In practice, the magi did have lords, and Vlod's lord was Edmund.

Koan's anchor was let go, splashing down, and the great ship backed hard, digging the flukes deep into the muddy bottom. A three to one scope was run out, the anchor cable snubbed, and the oars secured. A black ball was hoisted to the tip of the signal yard and secured there.

"We're here," Edmund announced.

Isham, *Koan's* new captain, was the first of the fleet's captains to arrive in the great cabin.

He reported on the river barge that had attracted their attention earlier, the one entering the Lewis River. She had been carrying weapons, bulk steel, bulk bronze, copper sheeting, and marine fittings.

At Wolfram's request for the details, Isham produced a list: bronze knees (hanging and lodging), mast rings, bronze gudgeons and pintles, nails, bolts, washers, nuts, and assorted other items of marine hardware. They were a sampling of the of fittings needed to build ships.

As for weapons, the list was less interesting: swords, knives, spear points, arrowheads, and similar mundane items—nothing out of the ordinary.

"Where were they offloaded?" Wolfram asked.

"At Vernon's new docks above Horseshoe Lake."

"Why not at Monticello itself?" Edmund asked. "Why not on the Cowlitz?"

"Has he established a new shipyard?" Wolfram asked.

Not wishing to open a previously closed debate but feeling compelled to nevertheless, Vlod said, "We've had reports."

Edmund frowned. "Shit."

"He's preparing for war," Wolfram.

"Only a fool doesn't," Edmund said.

"True enough."

Isham was thanked for his report and asked to wait for the other captains to arrive.

Wolfram and Edmund fell into a conversation about family matters, and Vlod went out onto the stern galley, which afforded him a view to the south across the Inner Harbor.

For the most part the fleet was moored, and a spectrum of their gigs, cutters, launches, and barges were threading their various ways toward the landing below Gilbert Hall.

In their wakes, they were leaving behind an equal spectrum of Seldon's boats. In general, they were tens, the sleek, powerful ten-oared scouting craft favored by the downriver clans for everything from scouting to surveying and from patrolling to light troop transport.

This evening, Seldon's tens were prowling among Edmund's ships, making a show of *helping* them to moor. Each of Seldon's tens was carefully shadowed by one of Edmund's own scouts.

And, too, there were also the bumboats, middle-sized row boats crammed with hawkers and harlots.

They wove expectantly in and out between the ships and made an ostentatious show of innocent commerce. No spies here. No, sir, not us. Look at this here, sir. Two for a penny! Look at 'em, sir. Can you believe it? Of course you can't, sir! You won't find their like in your home parts, will you, sir? No, of course you won't.

The tens and the bumboat boats hedged in Edmund's fleet. The agents they carried recorded the name and rig of the ships, their trim and deck cargoes. It was done with the same lack of modesty that the harlots flaunted themselves. The harlots, the genuine ones, were comparatively honest, comparatively moral.

Just at that moment, a new but related train of thought crossed Vlod's mental path and led him off in its traces. The tens and bumboat boats were as freshly painted as the harlots.

Vlod drew open the glass he had brought from the quarterdeck. Seldon's fifteens, which were a much heavier version of the tens, shadowed the action in and around the fleet, but they kept their distance. They were as crisp as the tens, freshly painted and freshly refitted.

It was a disturbing bit of information, but there was one welcome aspect to it. Edmund wouldn't have to worry about what Seldon was doing with the extra pocket money he was earning from his armament sales to Vernon.

To whom else was Seldon selling?

To whom could he sell? How big were his workshops? How robust were his supplies of raw materials? Skilled workers?

The fifteen Vlod had at first taken for the likely recipient of a fresh coat of paint swung through his field of vision, and the enormity of his mistake in lending any credit to that possibility leapt out at him through the glass.

The boat's planking was smooth and whole, without the irregularities of patching or replacement. The rails, fittings, and bright work were without blemish or scar. The oars were straight and free of weathering, and their blades were without damage. The ropework on the tiller was smart and sharp, unclogged by repeated coats of paint. There were no reddish-brown marks where rust had bled through the paint, or dark patches where the paint had been stained from within.

The fifteen was new!

He checked as many of Seldon's ships as possible and decided that a third of them were new. Ships weren't cheap. Seldon had to be spending his pockets empty, and his boots besides.

The next question introduced itself: why was Seldon building at such a breakneck speed?

For the same reason Vernon was, naturally.

They both expected a war and didn't want to be caught with their pants down.

Fine.

Narmer's ambitions were no secret.

The Cathedral's military weakness was no secret.

The inherent weakness of Edmund's fleet was no secret.

And neither was Vlod's cannon. Never mind that he had destroyed it and had, as far as anyone was aware, turned his research over to the Cathedral.

What had been done, could be done again.

Rather than settle matters once and for all, Vlod's cannon had aggravated the threat.

Vlod ought to have seen the potential, but he hadn't.

Another gloss reared its ugly head.

Thanks to the cannon, had Edmund replaced Narmer as the principal threat to the lower river? Was the building aimed at Edmund rather than at Narmer?

Ought to have. Could have been. Might have been. Maybe. If.

Where did the danger lie?

They were in shoal water, and in his zeal to secure Dagna's marriage to Gregory, Edmund had thrown the leads overboard.

Wolfram had tried to warn him. Vlod had tried to persuade him against it. They had failed. He had ordered the intelligence networks within Vernon's court and on his lands dismantled.

If Edmund had left them intact, they would be able tell him whether the rumors were rumors or whether they were facts. Intelligent action would be possible.

As things were, they were without eyes and ears. They were left to guess, and of all things, making guesses in matters of state was the most dangerous, both to Edmund and to Vernon.

Spies are not altogether bad things to have in one's employ, nor is it altogether unwise to invite your enemy's spies into your own councils.

Which was what made people like Ziellottes invaluable.

NINE

The day had slipped into late afternoon before the last of Edmund's captains had reported and received his instructions, before the galley and the fleet were moored to Wolfram's satisfaction.

With the late afternoon slipping into evening, Edmund shifted his household to the apartments provided for him in the main wing of the manor house, Gilbert Hall.

The hall bore the dual distinction of being the island's oldest continuously occupied building and of being its largest building. The second was a consequence of the first's not being entirely accurate. Over the centuries, the chieftains of Clan Sauvie had treated the hall to multiple waves of remodeling and expansion. What had begun as a timber and log building had been transformed into a stone and brick fortress, and from a fortress into a fortified manor house. Could a change to palace be far behind?

Vlod had studied several of the building's older drawings. They showed a modest stone keep and a diminutive curtain hall. They were impressive structures for their era, livable and battle-worthy, but the years and the growth in the island's prosperity had eclipsed them.

In part.

The habit of mind that had built and maintained the original curtain wall had not left the fate of the keep, and with it the fate of the manor holder, and with him the fate of the manor, to chance.

Nor had that habit of mind flaunted its innermost preparations to prevent a military disaster. At first glance, the keep appeared to be a glowering and looming part of the hall. It was not. Although they touched at several points, the structures were separate. The island's encompassing curtain wall might be breached, the Great Gate of Shillapoo smashed, the fleet sunk, and the hall and the town burned, but the keep would stand and hold for as long as needs be.

The inevitable irony was that the very commerce that the hall enabled was destroying it.

Edmund's suite of rooms was large, well appointed, and overlooked the Inner Harbor. Seldon had provided a sideboard laid with the traditional welcoming foods: wine, cheese, cream, salt, and bread. Each of them was of the finest quality. The wine and cheese were old and expertly aged, the bread and cream were fresh, and the salt was from Edmund's own saltworks, as Vlod was able to discern from the milling of the grains.

After seeing to Edmund's wants from the sideboard, Vlod poured himself a glass of wine and sliced off a wedge of cheese. He wrapped the cheese in a slice of bread.

The wine was from one of Seldon's wineries and had a slightly dull taste, but the cheese had the unmistakable sharp purity that was the envy of every manor up and down the river. Seldon's dairymen, along with everyone else's, had yet to duplicate it.

Such cheese had only one possible source: Phelan's dairies.

Phelan was a mountain chieftain, the leader of Clan Barlow. He was a loner and professed neutrality in whatever disputes raged back and forth across the lowlands.

He was in part a warrior, but mostly he was an entrepreneur. His lands lay between the Academy of Archmagus Basil the Anchorite and Wonderworker and the Brethren territories.

As Phelan's cheese dissolved in Vlod's mouth, the question of money, quite appropriately, came to mind. As with everything else to which he had set his intellect in the last few hours, there were no solid answers to be had, and no firm information upon which to speculate, and yet, his thoughts worked of their own volition, conveying him along as though he were a passenger on his own mental processes.

Was Phelan, a one-time enemy of Edmund's, lending money to Seldon? Was Seldon bringing something besides cheese down from Phelan's lair on the high slopes of Mt. Hood? Was it working capital, the money needed to build factories and to buy raw materials, or was it pocket money, the money needed to buy concubines, rare wines, tapestries, and assorted baubles? Or was it the money needed to build ships and to recruit and equip armies?

It was the latter, surely. The new bottoms proclaimed as much, openly and loudly.

Maybe.

Phelan's money, especially in large amounts, came with a price over and beyond the rates he charged. He demanded, and was invariably given, a voice in how his money was spent. Usually, his voice ensured that his money was used wisely, that is, used to make more money. He was generous with his sums and rates, but he was equally generous with his determination that the sums he lent be paid back at the rates agreed.

As well he should be, for he earned his cash, the money he hired out. He did not conquer it, nor did he extract it from his tenants. No, he earned it. He made it with his own sweat and his own wits.

He had begun his rise to wealth after losing a war to Edmund. Phelan had begun with slaves. At first his deals had been small, his skills uncertain, and his profits meager; but he had covered his costs, and a change in his fortunes for the better had come.

He had learned, and he had widened his scope of activity until his interests covered every aspect of slaving, from buying or capturing wild stock, to reselling, to breaking and training, and to financing and outfitting those who wished to try their hands at dealing with the Brethren directly, as Bevan and Fahraq did.

Slaving was not a hard or dangerous trade, despite having its moments, but neither did it have the safety and surety of fishing, farming, commercial trade, mining, and manufacturing. As a consequence of his desire to widen his range, to take part in this "safety and surety" on a scale that justified the financial risks, Phelan, in addition to hiring out his own money, also hired out that of other chieftains, pledging his personal wealth and that of his clan against any loss of their principal, a unique strategy that brought clients flocking to his banking houses.

Phelan had worked hard and he had bargained hard. He had done better by losing his war with Edmund than he would have done by winning it, and for his part, Edmund had gained nothing from his victory but another strong and cunning commercial competitor.

In the course of things, Phelan had made himself into a commercial powerhouse of sorts, if not a military one.

Well and good, but was he hiring out large sums of money to Seldon, and if he were, on what terms?

Despite the apparent logic of the situation—that Seldon was borrowing money from Phelan and using that money to expand his fleet—Vlod had no readily available way to determine whether he had discerned the truth.

Vlod finished his impromptu sandwich, and smiled. Phelan's cheese was beyond question.

The first of the porters arrived from the galley, and while they carried up the trunks, Brenna shepherded them in and out of the suite. She had wanted a squad of marines to do the porting, but Seldon's major-domo had politely but firmly established that it was "incumbent" upon his staff to perform such "menial tasks."

The major-domo instructed one of the adolescents in attendance upon him to light the gas lamps. Then, once the lamps were burning, he checked them to be sure that Edmund, a thoroughgoing rustic, would not be left to the mercies of wicks and wax.

That duty behind him, the major-domo bowed deeply, an understanding smile on his face.

"By the way," Edmund said, "what was that business with opening the Great Gate? It seemed to take forever."

"My lord, my lord Seldon wished me to convey his sincerest apologies. The gate's mechanism suffered a malfunction, and it took longer than expected to correct it." He smiled. "Please accept my apologies for not conveying my lord's apologies immediately. The press of business, you understand, my lord."

Edmund was itching to lop the weasel's head from his shoulders.

"The next time you find it necessary to hold us outside, send a signal,"

Edmund said. "Without a signal we can only imagine that we're being made sport of."

"Oh, no, my lord," the major-domo said. "I assure you, my lord, that the malfunction was quite genuine. A broken pin. A gear that refused to engage."

"Very well," Edmund said.

"Thank you, my lord. Most generous of you, my lord. Enjoy your evening, my lord. I hear the banquet will be spectacular, my lord."

"I'm sure it will be," Edmund said. "I would expect nothing less from my brother in the Harmony."

"Thank you, my lord," the major-domo said.

He bowed absurdly low, smiled too broadly, and left too greasily.

Edmund and Vlod went out onto the suite's balcony.

The sun was lowering, noticeably earlier than it had the week before.

"Did you notice the new fifteens, my lord?" Vlod asked.

"Seldon has a lot that's new," Edmund said. "I'm beginning to feel like an impoverished country mouse."

A metallic sound caught their attention. Down on the quay below Edmund's apartments, a troop of Seldon's guards were lighting the night torches lining McNary's Anchorage, a snug basin that opened off the Inner Harbor. They marched in rigid formation, the rasp of their boots harsh in the evening air.

A gang of men was working on the freight dock, the only one within a hundred meters of the hall. Under the direction of an overseer, the gang was manhandling the last of the mooring lines put over by one of Edmund's merchant galleys, the *Pride of Westport*.

At Edmund's request, the harbor master had arranged for *Pride* to be berthed as near to the hall as possible.

Ever the considerate host, Seldon had suggested putting her in McNary's Anchorage along with his personal barge and Edmund's cutter.

The overseer's curses were loud and brittle, out of place and out of proportion. Through the glass, Vlod looked at the men's faces. They were furrowed with hatred.

But for whom was their hatred? For their overseer? That answer rang true, but first answers tended to be wrong. For their work, then? Too wide of the mark.

The sort of labor they were doing didn't classify as work; it was brute labor, forced upon them either by the circumstances of their lives or by choices that had run foul.

For Seldon? For Edmund? For themselves?

Vlod washed the possibilities, as though he were washing gravel in a gold pan. The answer that stuck, that showed color, was that their hatred may have once had an object but that it no longer did. It had degenerated into an unfocused condition, one to which they had become utterly numb. It was no longer a conscious emotion, but an unexperienced, unseen foundation of those men's lives.

The laborers' faces were furrowed in hatred, yes; but they were unaware of it, much less were they aware of the causes for the furrowing.

Mirrors would be of no use. They would see their faces, recognize them as their own, although older than the last time they had paused to look at them, and then they would put down the mirrors and move on. Ship after ship, day after day, until finally they came to the end.

From the entryway on the far side of Edmund's apartments, the battle-master called, "Edmund?"

Pitching his voice to carry, Edmund answered, "Vlod and I are out here. Have you seen the sunset?"

Joining them, Wolfram said, "I've been keeping an eye on that daughter of yours."

"Which one?"

"The one who's about to skewer the chief porter."

"Brenna," Edmund said. "Protective child, my elder daughter. What's upset her?"

"Nothing to worry about. She might not kill him."

"You hope," Vlod said, lightly.

The lines in Wolfram's face—it was turning out to be an evening to mark the lines in people's faces—were deeper than they had been the day before, and the gray patches under his eyes were darker.

The stay at Seldon's, with its promises of quiet and genial pampering, was what he needed to recuperate. Without a doubt, he needed rest more than he needed the illusion of security he was buying with his exhaustion.

"The wine's quite good," Vlod suggested.

"Please."

Vlod went to the sideboard, poured a large glass, and heaped a plate with bread and cheese. When he returned to the balcony, Wolfram was saying, "I've cleared out Seldon's guards, and our own troops are securing the area." Between swallows of wine, he added, "Have you checked the rooms for listeners, spy holes, and the like?"

Vlod said, "After the porters are out of the way."

Wolfram leaned against the stone railing, his back to the harbor. "I'd rather have chosen a suite at the last minute."

Edmund smiled. "Why make extra work for Seldon's agents? They'd have to rig this entire wing every time they expected company."

"Don't!" Wolfram said, sardonically. "I'll break into tears."

"What makes you think they haven't rigged the entire wing already?" Vlod asked.

They laughed at his joke.

Edmund nodded his agreement.

Gesturing vaguely at a row of workshops and storehouses on the southern side of the anchorage, Edmund said, "If I were Seldon, I'd put my listeners over there."

The location was, without question, ideal for those ingenious mechanical snooping devices. Shaped like large, shortened trumpets, they had no moving parts, apart from their swivel mounts. Their large bells gathered in the sound, while their tubular extensions concentrated and directed it into an outlet attached to the earphones worn by their operators.

The size of the bell determined the listener's effective range, and the distance across the anchorage to the sheds was well within the capabilities legally permitted to the devices. What was done in practice was another matter entirely.

Wolfram said, "Shall I have them ripped out?"

"Make sure of them, but don't interfere. They'll know we know they're there, and that being the case, they won't be able to rely on anything we say." He smiled. "As things are, they'll have to keep on listening, anyway, the poor devils."

"A magus in the making," Vlod said, complimenting his chieftain with self-directed humor.

"I'll remember you said that."

Wolfram said, "I'd like to assign *Northern Star* to operate with Seldon's river command. A minor disturbance was reported up on the Little William, and they've asked if we want to tag along."

"Tag along to where?" Edmund asked. "To above or to below the quarry lands?"

"Above."

Edmund chewed on this. "No matter," he said. "In all hospitality, they ought to go. But take care that *Northern Star* is suitably impressed with our host's river navy."

Edmund's comment was for the listeners, not for Wolfram. Those, surely, would have been the battlemaster's instructions to *Northern Star* without Edmund's having told him. The phrase "river navy," too, would not be lost on Seldon when it was reported to him.

"Impressed, it is," Wolfram said.

"By the way," Edmund said, "have one of the larger biremes move farther out into the harbor and take up a station near the gate. *Ocean Dancer*, I think. I want her far enough off not to cause alarm, but close enough to preclude surprises."

"Cleared for action?"

"No, but have the catapults limbered and the crews standing by belowdecks. One last twist, have two of the scouts slip away and see what's to be seen, inside in the harbor and outside on the river."

"I see you don't care for the smell of the air, either," Wolfram said. "My apologies for not anticipating you."

"Never mind apologies. You're not free to offend Seldon, but I am… within limits."

"Agreed," Dagna said, and handed over her letter to Gregory. It was now wrapped in plain paper and closed against tampering by an ordinary wax seal.

The hostler of the Ax and Mace slid the packet inside his jerkin and held out his hand, palm up.

Dagna thumbed a heavy silver coin into it. "The rest after you've delivered it into *his* hands."

The Ax and Mace was neither the most nor the least reputable inn on Seldon's island, and the hostler had the look of one who's character matched his surroundings.

"I shall do as you say," he said, his voice too much a parody of mercantile reliability.

"No tricks, my friend." She grasped his arm and pressed her fingertips into a nerve bundle. The man's face paled almost immediately. "No sharp practice."

"No. No tricks. No practice."

"Good," Dagna said. "Because if there are, I will learn of them and then I will return to you and collect the debt you'll owe me."

She let go of his arm and walked out of the inn's stable.

In the street, she ignored the man who trailed along behind her. He had followed her from the quay to the Ax and Mace, and he was about to have the pleasure of following her down to Gilbert Hall. He was Aelman, one of her uncle Wolfram's better people, a bodyguard. He was pleasant company, too, when she was in the mood; but she wasn't in the mood, and so she left him to drag along behind without inviting him to join her. It was petty in its way, or maybe not. Often the best way to ensure one's safety was to appear vulnerable. In any case, it wasn't far to the hall, where he could leave her safety to her father's guards, and she could ask her uncle why Aelman had been assigned to watch over her.

While the sky was darkening in the west, Wolfram's people searched Edmund's suite for "listening tubes, spy holes, and the like."

None were found.

It was a good sign, especially coming as it did on the heels of that business with the Great Gate of Shillapoo. Had that chaos resulted from incompetence on the harbor master's part, or had it been a deliberate insult on Seldon's part?

Edmund suspected the latter but would hold himself ready to accept the former, publicly.

"Hospitality is not entirely dead," Edmund observed to Wolfram, and using hand gestures conveyed that the search was to be repeated later that night.

Wolfram nodded, and said, "No, it's not."

The last of the evening wind died, the traffic stilled, and the harbor became an undisturbed mirror.

"It must be almost time to go down to the banquet."

"What about the Gilbert River?" Wolfram asked, turning his back to the harbor and pitching his voice very softly.

The Gilbert was a shallow track of water that flowed out from the northwest corner of the Inner Harbor. As it snaked its way northward, it turned and twisted behind and between Seldon's foundries and armories, his smelters and heavy workshops. After covering a distance of four and a half kilometers, it emptied into the Holbrook Channel.

"Yes, what about the Gilbert?" Vlod chimed in, his voice matching Wolfram's. "Those new fifteens, they might not mean anything, or they might mean everything."

Wolfram raised an eyebrow, not in reproof but in agreement.

"Send a cutter from one of the merchant galleys," Edmund said. "Liberty parties tend to stray. Have some of your people mingle with the crew. I want a full report."

"What are they looking for?" Wolfram asked.

"Your people will know it when they see it," Edmund said.

Wolfram called a man-at-arms in from the passageway. They talked for a few moments, and the man departed.

Returning to the balcony, Wolfram said, "We'll have a report after the banquet."

The harbor reflected the light of the torches on the quays framing the anchorage, and the images of Gilbert Hall and the keep floated on its surface.

Wolfram's man-at-arms crossed the quay, climbed into a boat and rowed out to *Wave Song*, the command ship for the scouts and picket boats.

"It's nearly time to go down to the hall," Edmund said unhappily.

As though in answer, the door from the passageway opened, and Brenna led a lieutenant under the command of Prokoffy, the commander of the shore guard, into the main room. His cloak was spattered with dried blood, and his face looked as though he had been riding hard for several hours.

Brenna called to her father and started out onto the balcony, but Edmund greeted her with familial banalities and motioned for her to stay where she was. He would come to them.

She motioned for the rider to stop where he was, and the chieftain led Wolfram and Vlod in from the balcony.

With an expression of cruel triumph in his eyes, Edmund put a finger to his lips, forbidding any genuine conversation in the room. He gestured to Wolfram, and the battlemaster embarked upon a stream of chatter. Brenna, Edmund, and Vlod picked it up, while the man in the cloak remained mute.

Without having to be told, Vlod handed a pen and paper to Prokoffy's officer.

The man scrawled a note and handed it to Edmund.

As the chieftain read through it, his expression changed from one of triumph to one of fixed resolve. He took up the pen, turned over the paper, and wrote. The words were large and filled the page. When he was done, he showed it to the officer.

A commotion broke out in the passageway beyond the door. The major-domo demanded admittance on a matter of the utmost importance.

The guards explained to him precisely how much weight his demands carried with them.

But surely their lord would wish to be made aware that Lord Seldon was ready to receive them, as appointed, in the great hall.

They promised to inform their lord.

But Lord Seldon had personally instructed him to deliver the message himself. How was he to return to Lord Seldon without completing his instructions?

He was in quite a pickle, wasn't he? Well, he might try walking. Or crawling! Ha, ha, ha!

"Wolfram, silence that," Edmund said.

The lieutenant gestured at the door. He had to return to Prokoffy without being noticed.

Edmund pointed at Brenna. "She'll get you clear," he murmured, low enough for any listeners that they may have missed to be unable to pick it up through the racket. Edmund touched the man's arm. "Tell Prokoffy that he must not fail me in this."

"No, my lord. He will not fail you," the rider said, and Brenna led him out of the apartments through a back exit.

Prokoffy's lieutenant would be anonymous, functionally hidden in the ebb and flow of Edmund's people.

Moments later, after the racket outside the door had abated, Brenna reentered the suite and made her report. "He's on his way."

"How far out are they?" Edmund asked.

"A klick or two. They'll arrive in time," she said. "We might not, though. They must be waiting for us."

An honor guard arrived to escort Edmund and his party into the great hall. Brenna's marines, in full dress uniform, their draw catches loosened, doubled Seldon's official escort.

The move raised eyebrows, but none of Seldon's people objected.

Within the rectangle of troops, Vlod, Warrick, and Royden led the way. Behind the magi came Dagna and Brenna. Both of Edmund's daughters were in court dress; however, Brenna was wearing her battle knife in plain view.

In court dress, Brenna's aspect as woman, as mistress of the most powerful manor on the Columbia, as the woman who occasionally shared Vlod's bed, ran freer than when she was in uniform, freer than when she was most herself, freer, oddly enough, than when they were making love. He had rarely seen her as beautiful. Her face was lightly made up, and her hair hung in a single leatherbound braid that extended down to the small of her back. The bodice of her dress, which was of embroidered linen, was also leather-bound, according to the custom and style of the downriver clans, to match the braid in her hair. At her left hip, her battle knife hung on a plain leather belt. The weapon's gold-and-silver scabbard was her only jewelry.

In turn, Edmund's daughters were followed by Wolfram, who was followed by Landis, acting in her capacity as principal dancer, and by the mother superior of Edmund's manor henge, and, finally, Edmund walked in the place of honor at the end of the procession.

The captain of Seldon's guard guided them out of the guest wing and down to the ceremonial doors to the great hall, which were closed pending Edmund's arrival.

The ceremonial doors were built of hewn oak timbers and banded with bronze. Copper bas-reliefs mounted between the bands depicted the more heroic events in the manor's history. The construction of the Great Gate of Shillapoo was prominently featured, extending into a second panel. The expression on the face of Shillapoo the Younger appeared to indicate his pleasure at having been afforded the extra room.

There was a brief squabble over seating and protocol, which Edmund settled, in part by asking his retinue where they wanted to sit.

With the dust settled, the door keeper sent a messenger into the hall, presumably to Seldon's major-domo both warning him of the changes and asking him for instructions.

Moments later, the door keeper's attendants swung open the doors, and an attendant motioned to the captain of the guard.

"Vlod, walk beside me," Brenna said. "See what I see."

At a signal from the captain of Seldon's guard, the door keeper announced Edmund's party, striking his staff on the floor slates 21 times, and they marched into the hall.

The bulk of Edmund's House and clan, those that Seldon and Edmund had invited to the welcoming banquet, were already seated, and at the announcement of their chieftain's name, they rose to their feet as one and cheered. The sound of it broke through the hall. It thundered along the walls, and it shook the pavements beneath Vlod's feet.

"Listen to them, Vlod!" Brenna whispered. "Do you hear it? The love of a warrior people!"

Vlod had no need of her explanation. They loved her father as she did, unstintingly and without compromise, and she was proud of them for loving him, and of him for drawing their love to himself and for loving them in return.

It was the loyalty of a chieftain sworn and given to his people. It was the blood loyalty of his warriors, earned by his courage, and sworn and given to him by them in answer.

It was the clan; it was the house; it was the coin and measure of their lives.

And the hall trembled with the might of it.

At Seldon's signal, his people rose to their feet and took up the cheer.

The escort melted away onto the flanks, and following the captain of Seldon's personal guard, Edmund's inner circle strode up the center of the hall toward the raised platform onto which the head of Seldon's U-shaped banquet table, the hall's high table, had been elevated.

Out of the corners of his eyes, Vlod noticed Wolfram's marines, close to the outside walls, pacing up the length of the cavernous room.

Seldon owned his hall, but it was Wolfram who was bringing it under control.

TEN

The Great Hall of Seldon's Manor could have amply contained four full-sized war galleys, oar tip to oar tip and stem to stern. The room was twice as long as it was wide, and the peaks of its rafters were hidden from view by the smoke rising from the fires.

The high table stretched the width of the hall and ran some meters down the sides. It was draped in white, and ornate, high-back chairs lined its outboard sides.

Starting within the bight of the "U", four rows of undraped tables, with benches, extended the length of the room.

Two circular fire pits, each of which was some two meters across, heated the center of the room, while braziers warmed the perimeter. The smoke escaped through mortared holes in the roof above the pits. The technique was a sentimental holdover from an earlier age.

Seldon was on the platform, an uncomfortable expression on his face. His eyes darted from Edmund, to Brenna, to Dagna, to the magi, to the marines keeping pace in the shadows, repeating the round several times.

Edmund's party halted, divided into two ranks, and Edmund advanced between them. In passing, he threw a warning look to Dagna, and a sterner one to Brenna.

Edmund stepped up beside his host, and Seldon opened the welcoming ritual. "My brother in the Harmony, we are well and truly met!"

When the two chieftains had finished reciting their meaningless platitudes about peace and honesty, Seldon's pages showed Edmund and his party to their places at the table.

They remained standing, and the members of Seldon's inner household joined them. The seating pattern resulted in the alternation of the members of the two houses.

Seldon and Edmund were given drinking horns. Another round of platitudes was recited, and the two chieftains interlocked their arms and, drinking to each other's prosperity, drained the horns.

The hall broke into cheers, cheers that lasted for several minutes.

Edmund's place was on Seldon's left, while on his right was Dagna's place, Brenna having chosen to be seated according to her standing within her father's court rather than according to her place within his family.

To Edmund's left was Flora, Seldon's wife, balancing Dagna, who was acting as mistress of Edmund's clan by default.

The next alternations encompassed the battlemasters, field commanders, and river commanders, with a vacant chair left where Prokoffy would have sat in the pattern had he been present, between Jürgen and Lamont, two of Seldon's rising military stars.

Then came the mothers superior and senior priestesses of the manor henges and temples. Landis was seated with this group, dressed in black and gold, her breasts fashionably exposed.

And hers were not the only naked breasts in evidence. Although far from general and far from accepted, the new dancer's style was creating many a quizzical glance, many a whispered comment, and many an inward estimation of possibility among the younger women of the two courts.

The senior magi comprised the next lower rank. Thaddeus and someone Vlod did not recognize represented Seldon's House, while Royden and Warrick represented Edmund's. Vlod had insisted before they entered that even though he was Edmund's personal magus, he was far junior to Royden and Warrick, was not the clan's official magus, much less its Rector of Magi and ought, therefore, to be seated farther down the table.

In Thaddeus's case, the title was a marker of status and power; in Royden's, it was functionally an honorific—by his own choice and by Edmund's. Thaddeus spent his days surrounded by lackeys and his own personal guard; Royden spent his days crawling around Edmund's shipyards and dockyards, and working among his armorers, engineers, blacksmiths, craftsmen, teachers, thinkers, and artisans, ensuring that their activities and plans fell within the established boundaries of technological propriety.

Thaddeus ruled within the scope Seldon allowed him and sometimes beyond it; Royden worked at whatever task came his way, within his ken or outside of it.

If Vlod was Edmund's eyes and if Wolfram was his armies, then Royden was his blacksmith, his shipwright, and his engineer rolled into one.

Alternations of commercial and agrarian functionaries followed, and, at last, far down the runs of the high table, came the final alternations of the two Houses.

Seldon's sister Xenia, Brenna, Tremayne, and Vlod were thrown together at the end of the run on Edmund's side of the high table.

Xenia's presence was intended as a balance to Brenna's. The set of Xenia's face betrayed her opinion of the arrangement, betrayed the emotional cost to her of being thrown into close proximity to Tremayne; while for her part, Brenna's face was open, pleasant, expectant, but unrevealing. It was the sort of face that Vlod had often seen her wear before going into battle, and it put him on his guard.

Tremayne's being seated at the table was the work of a subtler touch than the one that had cast Xenia from the social heights.

Tremayne was one of Seldon's junior magi and a close friend of Vlod's. A few years older than Vlod, he had begun his studies with Vlod's father at the age of ten. At the unheard-of age of twelve, he had passed his entrance exams and had been admitted to the Academy.

The next year, Vlod's father had been burned at the stake for heresy, but, luckily, none of the stigma of heresy had attached to Tremayne.

Nevertheless, stigma or no stigma, his career had languished, at least as judged by courtly position and the power that went along with it. No, such delights were not for the likes of Tremayne, burrowing Tremayne, digging Tremayne, Tremayne the Mole, Tremayne the Magpie, Tremayne the Scribbler. Poor lad, he'd have to content himself with curating a neglected museum full of forgettable and forgotten junk. It was his own damn fault. No doubt he'd breathed in too much dust! Hahaha!

Vlod was Edmund's personal magus, and because of it, he was considered to socially outrank his friend. Thus, on the one hand, Tremayne's being seated next to Vlod was a gesture of good will on Seldon's part: the two were fast friends, and would have much to discuss. On the other hand, Tremayne was junior to Vlod in social rank, despite his technical seniority as a magus, and thus, the seating was a double insult of sorts, a challenge to Edmund to stop playing the democrat, and a warning to Vlod that he was in danger of overstepping that which was allowed to hatchlings, no matter what their connections and service were.

A knack, dear boy, for flamboyant technologies tends to give people the hives.

Running this train of thought to ground while he waited for the two chieftains to finish their mutual greetings, Vlod decided that he was, perhaps, discerning malevolence and threat where there were none. Such was a dangerous undertaking; however, had he undertaken such an exercise nine or ten months ago, Edmund's heir might well be alive instead of rotting in the mud at the bottom of the river.

As soon as the chieftains "well-and-truly-met" ritual was completed, the guests were allowed to sit.

Once seated, Vlod, Tremayne, and Brenna fell to catching up with a vengeance.

In response to yet another one of Tremayne's stories about his never-ending search for artifacts, Vlod asked, "Have you ever found one intact?"

Tremayne shrugged. "If I ever do, if I ever find one that isn't rusted solid with most of its parts gone, I'll figure out how they worked, and if I can do that, then..."

"Then what?" Brenna asked.

"I'll have found the keys to the kingdom."

Vlod listened as Tremayne outlined his plans for his next series of digs: a pre-Winter graveyard, a possible manufacturing plant, and a fortified encampment that was likely constructed in the immediate post-Winter period.

Try as he would, Vlod could not concentrate on Tremayne's plans.
Why?

Because Seldon's banquet was beguiling, intriguing, mesmerizing. It was a puzzle that called out to Vlod for solution, if such a thing were within the scope of his talents.

There was, for example, Seldon's sister, Xenia. She was dressed in a silk gown that both hugged her body and flowed loosely about her from neck to toe like a pale green and yellow aura. She was a handsome woman in her late thirties, with flowing hair and bright, cold eyes.

She was an intimate of Her Beatitude, the Most Blessed Ulricka, Mother Metropolitan of the Inland Empire and the Holy Oregon, whose Cathedral was the Cathedral Henge of Eileen the Immortal.

The Cathedral was the mother henge of the manor and shrine henges, the temples, retreat houses, religious communities, and hermitages throughout the Columbia River Basin and for a considerable distance beyond. Xenia had endowed many of the retreats, communities, and hermitages herself, and she spared scant effort to keep their populations growing.

Closer to home, she guided the activities of a vague but powerful clique of priestesses and hangers-on within Seldon's court. About this, doubt was *not* possible, despite the regularly promulgated information to the contrary.

Further, her power was reported to extend into the ranks of her brother's senior magi, and through them, into the Academy. About this, doubt *was* possible, but considered to be unwise.

Vlod was far from sanguine about sitting anywhere within a hundred meters of the woman, but Brenna, long-since bored with Tremayne's recitation, was chatting with her as though the two of them were reunited sisters who had been separated years before by two unhappy marriages.

Changing subjects, Xenia asked Brenna, "Do you enjoy the military life?"

"Why wouldn't I?"

"I can't speak for you, but I'd find it limiting."

"I don't."

As luck would have it, Xenia's answer was silenced by the beating of drums at the far end of the hall.

"Ah, here's the entertainment. They're quite good."

The ceremonial doors swung open and a troop of Asian acrobats entered in a flurry of brightly colored costumes, to the accompaniment of a frenetic fanfare played on flutes, drums, and a dozen instruments that Vlod could not name.

The troop juggled and tumbled across the rows of tables, working their way into the open space in front of the high table.

Ten of the acrobats formed a pyramid, with an eleventh standing on the shoulders of the one at the apex. A twelfth stood in position before the structure and begged for Seldon's permission to entertain him.

Not unexpectedly, it was granted, and the eleventh acrobat dove from the apex, somersaulted, and landed on her feet on the twelfth's shoulders.

The pyramid dissolved in a hail of tumbling bodies, and reformed into the next geometric design.

In the midst of a six-person juggling routine, the ceremonial doors crashed open, and Prokoffy strode into the great hall. He was at the head of two dozen of his best troops. Their boots were caked with mud, their cloaks were spattered with it, and they had drawn their weapons.

Prokoffy carried a round, cloth-wrapped bundle in one hand, and his sword in the other.

With a dismissive shout, the commander of Edmund's shore guard used the flat of his steel to repel one of Seldon's guards, a man who had proven himself stupid enough to attempt to stop the advance toward the high table.

Wolfram's people secured the perimeter in a single movement. The evolution was quiet and deadly. Best of all, it had gone unknown and unsuspected by Seldon's guards until it was done.

Throughout the hall, laughter and sighs of delight stammered off and died. The acrobats scattered before the commander's searing advance.

Prokoffy's boots hammered on the floor. The sound of it thundered along the walls and up into the vault of the ceiling.

Prokoffy came to a halt a dozen paces in front of the high table. His men-at-arms formed a semicircle behind him. With their backs to their commander, they faced the assembly. They pointed their swords outward toward the hall.

By this time, Seldon and Edmund were on their feet.

Brenna whispered to Vlod, "Well done!"

The commander held the bundle out in front of him. "My Lord Edmund!" he called, and tossed the bundle in a steep arc toward the high table.

Because he had held on to one end of the cloth wrapping, as the bundle rose, it trailed behind a long, narrow strip of blood-stained fabric. The streamer rippled and billowed as it ran out.

The bundle passed through its apex, and left behind the last of its wrapping. The object revealed fell, naked, onto the floor, making a hollow sound as it struck.

It bounced and rolled forward.

It struck the base of the dais directly below Edmund's feet.

Prokoffy announced, "Fahraq, the Chieftain of Clan Nehalem, requests an audience!"

The head spun around and came to rest with its sightless eyes gaping up toward Edmund. There was no mistaking the horror in them.

Seldon's wife, Flora, screamed, and Dagna, who was seated at the high table in the place designated for the mistress of Edmund's household, assumed her most disgusted expression.

Seldon demanded, "By what right—"

"Hold your tongue, sir!" Edmund commanded.

Prokoffy cast aside the winding cloth, and in one movement, he lifted the head on the point of his sword and offered it to his chieftain.

Grasping the head by the hair, Edmund lifted it from the sword, and held it aloft. The mouth dropped open, and a trickle of dark fluid dribbled onto the table.

Xenia glanced across the distance at Dagna. Their eyes met and locked. Xenia was the first to look away. She made a show of gagging and swept from the hall.

Addressing the banquet, Edmund said, "Fahraq was my trusted ally, but he betrayed me. He conspired in the assassination of my grandson!"

There was a general murmur of disbelief, of a rough acceptance of the fact that such behavior merited such treatment.

"Mark his fate!" Edmund said.

He regarded the head for a long second, then he threw it to the dogs on the far side of the hall.

Dagna left her place and exited through the same door that Xenia had taken.

The dogs yelped and scrambled away from Fahraq's head as it fell among them, but the instant it had stopped rolling, they snarled and barked and snapped at one another, fighting for its possession.

In a single wave, Edmund's people rose to their feet and cheered their lord. The ovation broke like an ocean wave and flooded the hall.

The ground was immediately washed from beneath Seldon's feet. Left with no other choice, he rose and applauded. Following his example, the members of his court joined their voices to those of Edmund's clan.

Seldon's guards tossed the head out through a side door, and then drove the bickering animals after it.

With the door closed, the dogs' snarling and barking were muted by the stone wall, but their underlying ferocity was not.

Edmund resumed his seat. The cheering stopped, and the clapping subsided.

Prokoffy's troops formed ranks, and their officer marched them out.

Stepping up onto the dais, Prokoffy sat next to Edmund, in the place Flora had vacated.

"Hard ride?" Edmund asked.

Prokoffy made a face. "Full of surprises."

"I can imagine."

An attendant appeared and offered the commander of the Shore Guard a bowl to wash his hands in.

Drying them, Prokoffy said to Edmund, "What's for dinner?"

The stewards changed the linens and utensils on the high table and poured fresh wine into clean glasses.

By the time they had finished, the banquet had regained its composure, and in a short time its festive mood returned. The acrobats resumed their routines, and Seldon began talking with Edmund as though nothing had happened to disrupt the flow of the evening.

Vlod felt Tremayne tap him on the shoulder.

"What is it?" Vlod asked.

"Bad move. Impressive, but bad."

"Why?"

"Not here," he said, and led Vlod out of the hall.

Dagna caught up to Xenia on a terrace that overlooked the inner harbor.

The two women studied each other for a moment.

Dagna was the first to speak. "Are you all right?" she asked. The question was pathetic, the solicitude ludicrous, but it would have to serve.

Seldon's sister Xenia smiled. "Why wouldn't I be?"

"Then why did you bolt?"

"Because I didn't care to sit through another one of your father's exhibitions. My brother may be impressed by that sort of nonsense, but I have little or no patience for it." Xenia laughed in amusement. "Mind you, my brother *was* impressed, the poor schlub."

"That was the whole point."

"Your father can't possibly hold my brother responsible for the petty rebellions among your father's hirelings."

"He can in part."

"That's a fish that won't swim."

"Won't it?"

"No, it won't," Xenia said.

The fencing had gone on far too long, and the ache where Dagna had torn during her delivery was vying for her attention. "Did you lead me out here to pick a fight?"

"I didn't lead you, you followed me."

"Perhaps I misunderstood. I thought that you'd *called* to me."

Xenia's eyes widened, but they instantly regained their normal size. "I did." Before Dagna could respond, Xenia added, "So it's true: you are adept. It stands to reason. Your mother was quite gifted. Her marriage to your father denied the then-Mother Metropolitan one of her greater strengths."

"That's ancient history. Why bring it up now?"

"You have many of her gifts."

Dagna sought to frame a denial, but the ground was undulating under her feet. She wished that she's stayed inside. In order to steady herself, in order to touch the earth, she rested her hand on the railing's stone. The ground moved sharply, and Dagna shifted more of her weight to it. She brought the cold, rough texture of the stone to the center of her mind.

Xenia's face took on an expression of surprise and concern. "You need to sit down," she said. "Come."

Dagna allowed herself to be guided onto a low bench.

The older woman's hands lingered on her shoulders, and her perfume, imported for her by her brother, was heavy in the night air. "They've used you without pity."

"Each of us is used," Dagna said. The night was cool for late summer, and despite the swirling in her head and the lightness in her arms and legs, Dagna could feel the woman's presence. The swirling was slowing. "In the end, duty uses us up."

"Don't presume to lecture."

"Don't pretend to be ignorant."

"A touch!" Xenia gave her a sidelong look. "Your mother broke free."

"You're wrong, there," Dagna said. "She traded one duty for another."

"But she chose the new one, didn't she?"

"She chose the old one, too. She was no one's pawn."

Suddenly, the whole space around them pitched violently. It corkscrewed to the left, then came back onto the level. Xenia was sitting too close to her, crowding her.

Dagna pulled away and risked standing up. The surge subsided, but she knew it would return. "I need to go in."

"You need to go to bed."

"Later."

"Spoken like the true and loyal daughter of a chieftain. But what does Dagna the woman have to say?"

"That I ought to go in."

"You have your father's courage and your mother's gifts," Xenia said. Her voice was soft, comforting. "The Goddess entrusted them to you. You ought to make better use of them."

"And?" It was her father's word, his way of saying it. The time either to counterattack or to retreat was upon her. "What do you want me to do?" she demanded, her voice sharp.

Unruffled, Xenia said, "I've been stalking you." Triumph lit Xenia's face. "Tonight I've flushed you. You didn't give a damn whether I was ill or not. You followed me out here because your father disgusts you. You hate him for what he and his enemies did to your child."

"I thought you were ill," Dagna said.

"No, my dear. You answered because you were hunting me."

"Why would I do that?" Dagna asked, challenging her.

"Because I know the name you gave to your murdered son!"

In one stroke, executed exactly as Prokoffy had taught her to execute it, without thought and at blinding speed, Dagna pinned Xenia to the wall of Gilbert Hall. Dagna's elbow pressed hard into the front quarter of the woman's neck.

"Let me explain your situation to you," Dagna said. "Right now, I could turn your larynx into so much bloody pulp if I choose to." Dagna fought the nausea rising to engulf her, accepted and dismissed the battle madness that sought to engulf her, the intoxicating lust for blood. "For the last time, Xenia, what do you want from me?"

"I wish to offer you justice and sanctuary."

The door through which Tremayne led Vlod opened onto an elegant, high-walled patio. Marble flower beds lined the perimeter, and a reflecting ball dominated the center.

Vlod asked, "Alright, why was it a bad move?"

"He's shown them his weakness."

"In what way? In avenging murder and treason?"

"Don't be silly! Treason and murder must be suppressed," Tremayne said. "No, he's shown them his need for a grandson."

"He can't shrug off an assassination!"

"Calm down," Tremayne said, acting the older brother. "Use your mind. He's thrown a temper tantrum, not exacted justice, and they can spot the difference."

"Carrion like Fahraq don't understand justice, but they do understand force."

"Fahraq?" Tremayne asked with heavy irony. "Was he your enemy?"

"What have you heard?"

"I don't have to have heard anything," Tremayne said. "Ask yourself, was Fahraq capable of arranging and executing a complex assassination?"

A sidestep! Why? What had Tremayne heard?

"We're looking into it."

"Here another question for you: did killing Fahraq kill the plot?"

This was firmer ground, and thankful for it, Vlod said, "You're asking me to betray the confidence of Edmund's House."

"I don't give a damn whether you answer me or not, but you damn well better have an answer for Edmund."

"Don't worry," Vlod said. "I have an answer."

Tremayne sighed in relief.

"One more thing," Tremayne said. "Unless I'm very wrong, their next attack will be on Dagna."

After being outside, to Vlod, the atmosphere inside the hall felt heavy and overheated. A troop of dancers was performing.

Vlod resumed his place at the table.

Brenna asked, "What was that about?"

"I'll tell you later," Vlod said, and watched the banquet, rather than the dancers.

Amidst the milling to and fro and the diffuse rumble of conversation, Seldon's stewards carried platters heaped with food along the tables. They bent to display the fare, and served the items requested.

Tremayne excused himself and left the hall.

Brenna and Xenia, who had returned to the banquet, were watching the dancers. Xenia was friendly with most of them, and privy to an inexhaustible supply of stories and rumors about their careers and private lives.

Dagna sat in her place at the high table, gray-faced and tight-lipped.

Vlod withdrew into himself, not to consider the truth of what Tremayne had told him, but to escape the ugliness around him.

He watched the dancers, not seeing them as individuals, but tracing the larger patterns of their routines. As energetic and distracting as the dancer were, Vlod was soon looking past the dancers and at Seldon's guests.

Although Edmund's people were present in number, the vast majority of those in the hall were from the Manor Island itself.

To Vlod, the hall was no longer a hall as such, but became a feedlot populated by stout, tidy manor dwellers. Their faces and bodies were round and slack. Their hands were stained with dye, polish, and ink. Their faces lined with commercial cunning.

Times change, Vlod lectured himself, and shifted his attention to the wine bearers. They were loosely dressed slave girls chosen for reasons more compelling than their knowledge of wine. Their master had wine stewards for that.

The wine bearers moved provocatively along the tables. They bent, joking, talking, smiling, bending low over the tables, hoping to catch the eye of a man with the money and the willingness to buy them away from Seldon's household. They balanced the tall wine jars on their hips, and poured, while they dreamed of wealth and freedom.

Good luck to them!

The stewards served from silver platters, and together with the wine bearers, they flowed in an unbroken stream from the kitchens. However, regardless of how many of them came, regardless of how strong the flood of food and drink was, the tidy, round burghers could not be filled.

They were a generation that schemed in safety. They were housed and sheltered behind stone walls and an army that had been built—and understood!—by those who had come before them.

Seldon I, the builder of the manor's original wooden and brick walls, had called for carrying the battle into the heart of the Brethren lands, into "the very bowels of the infection." He had railed against peace and accommodation and "working together for the common good." He had preached the need to fill the rivers and creeks with Brethren blood. He had vowed to light his victory fires on the summit of their mounded corpses.

Seldon III, the current chieftain of Clan Sauvie, spoke in carefully moderated tones of crop prices, his beloved silkworms, the coming harvest, the transit fees he paid to Edmund, the current fashions in court dance, the mistresses he kept, the wife he loved, and of his collection of tapestries.

He spoke of weapons, too, of what was possible and of what was not, but behind closed doors.

Only in the middle of the night did he exchange whispers with his commanders about Edmund's secret ambitions and Vlod's cannon.

He comforted himself with the dual reminder that the plans for that cannon, for that abomination of fire and shot, were locked away in Ulricka's archives and that she would never have the stomach to build one of the ghastly things.

ELEVEN

After the banquet, Edmund called his inner circle together in the great cabin aboard *Koan*. It was the only place they could be sure of, within limits. Seldon and his people were nothing if not inventive when it came to spying.

His opening question went to the quick: "Why wasn't Fahraq taken alive? The details."

The cabin was dark except for the double-wicked lamp hanging above the table.

Its yellow-orange light slanted down across Prokoffy's face. "The place was in a shambles. It looked as though Fahraq had been trying to put down a coup...or the opening attack of a civil war."

"Go on."

"We were recognized at the gate and taken to him. I arrested him in your name, and he chose to fight." Prokoffy pointed at his own neck. "An arrow caught him in the neck. None of us shot it." Prokoffy made an open-handed movement. "He was as good as dead before he hit the ground."

Wolfram made a sarcastic noise in his throat. "He was as good as dead before you left camp, unless I'm wrong."

Edmund waved his brother to silence. "Whose arrow was it? One of his?"

"No, and it wasn't one of ours."

"Whose, then?"

"Can't say. New style, though. Maybe Brethren."

"He was silenced," Edmund said.

"By whom?" Wolfram asked, developing the argument.

"The people who attacked the fleet," Edmund said. "What happened after he was killed?"

"I took his head. Thought it would make an impressive souvenir. We captured his battlemaster, Ransom the Walleyed."

"His condition?"

"He'll recover."

Connecting the dots, Edmund asked, "Was he injured when you took him into custody?"

Prokoffy's expression hardened a notch. "We pulled him out of one of the Fahraq's watchtowers." He left a deliberate pause. "It was in flames at the time. We saved his life."

"Again, what's his condition?"

"Badly burned. One or two minor sword cuts. If he doesn't infect too badly, he'll live."

"Very well. Go on."

"We had to fight our way out," Prokoffy said. "Their hearts weren't in it, though. Chickens-in-the-barnyard stuff."

A smirk turned through a corner of Brenna's mouth. "Fahraq was hardly well loved."

Vlod drew a wavy line with his finger on the table in front of him. A line of poetry came to him from his childhood, *He left it dead, and with its head he went galumphing back.* But, head or no head, Edmund wasn't likely to be the one of whom it could be said that *He chortled in his joy!*

To Prokoffy, Edmund said, "You've laid a victory at my feet that isn't mine to claim."

"You were right to pick it up, my lord," Prokoffy said. "We've taken advantage of a situation not of our own making, like using a rainstorm to cover an attack. Call what we've done a ruse of war. The basin will believe that you killed Fahraq, and that belief will act as cover for whoever did. He will feel confident of his safety, and it will be that same confidence that will betray him. And when it does, we will be there, standing ready to greet him."

"You're hoping they—whoever they are—will fuck up," Wolfram said.

"With respect, Wolfram, no, I'm not counting on Edmund's enemy to make a mistake. I'm planning to take advantage of his self-satisfaction. I'm planning to exploit his character."

Never before had Vlod heard the Commander of the Shore Guard reveal so much of his approach to combat, or of the inner workings of his mind.

His tone newly speculative, Wolfram said, "First Valeda and now Fahraq. Somebody is brushing out his tracks."

"Agreed," Edmund said, "but who?"

"Why do we keep asking the same old question?" Brenna said. "It was Bevan!"

Turning back to Prokoffy, Edmund asked, "What was the state of things when you left?"

"Messy," Prokoffy said. "The keep was on fire by the time we were two klicks out."

"Tell me about the fires," Edmund said.

"Not our work, and the people with Fahraq weren't throwing it around. The fires could have been set by the same people who assassinated Fahraq."

"Covering move," Brenna said.

"Or an oil lamp that got tipped over in the fighting," Wolfram said.

Edmund dismissed everyone but Vlod.

When they were alone, Edmund said, "Before you hammer your brains into mush trying to prove it, the culprit wasn't Bevan, nor was it Vernon. Bevan doesn't take risks, and Vernon is never, never, ever lax."

"Meaning what?"

"Meaning that we have another hand in play."

"Yes, my lord," Vlod said. Bevan's was the only hand with anything immediate to gain, and Vernon was off his game.

Edmund said, "Before we question Ransom, I want you to go hunting."

The very next morning, Tremayne rode with Vlod as far as Seldon's northern boundary and arranged with the guards for him to be passed out and allowed to reenter with a minimum of fuss.

While Vlod was sliding the transit permits into an inside pocket, Tremayne asked, "All right, what are you up to and how can I help?"

"I'm going hunting." Patting each piece, he recited his list of equipment. "I have my spear, my bow, arrows, long sword, battle knife, ax, rope, bedroll, a change of clothes, and provisions for several days."

"Hunting?" Tremayne asked, as though it were the least likely of explanations. "You're going to stick to hunting?"

"Don't be too quick," Vlod said. The gate closed behind them, and the crossbar rasped into place. "I bested Dagna last year."

"She must have been sleeping with her eyes open."

"Hungover." Vlod continued: "She woke up one morning and realized who she'd married and began drinking. She didn't stop until she passed out."

"Poor girl."

"Poor Gregory."

"I thought they were in love," Tremayne said.

"They were, but that doesn't mean Dagna didn't have a rude awakening."

"Most married people do."

"Most *people* do."

The road leading from the gate angled up and away from the river, traversing a bare side hill. The day was cool without being cold, and clear but with a spattering of high clouds. The Columbia was blue and painfully bright in the morning sun. The wind was kicking up out on the water, but it was sedate ashore owing to the trees and the topography.

At the moment, Tremayne and Vlod were in a wind shadow, but higher up, Vlod would have the full force of it.

Tremayne reined in his horse, while Vlod's walked on. "Hunt well, my friend, and remember to come back with a deer."

Vlod twisted in his saddle and waved. "If you don't see me in ample time for the Stone Builder's Birthday Party, you may assume that I was eaten by wild dogs."

Tremayne laughed. "There may be more truth there than you might wish!"

Vlod waved to his friend, feeling as though he were looking at him for the last time, not that anything would happen to Tremayne, but that Vlod might be killed.

The idea was pure nonsense.

Well, it was mostly pure nonsense.

The Brethren might be around, but it wasn't likely. Furthermore, whoever had been pulling Fahraq's strings, they would have cleared out the moment the man had died. Thus, contrary to his doubts, Vlod was convinced that he'd have his travels to himself.

Dropping his arm from a final wave, he spurred his horse forward. The Stone Builder's Birthday Party was in five days. In five days Vlod would either have answers to their questions or he would be dead.

Over his shoulder, he saw Tremayne wheel around and make for the gate.

After the two magi had gone their separate ways, one of the border guards, a corporal, suggested to his sergeant that fresh venison sounded like a good idea. That little magus had something there! The sergeant recalled the salt beef they had boiled up the night before and agreed to let the man go hunting. He was to be gone for a very few hours at most.

The corporal took his bow and quiver arrows and set out on horseback. He followed a side road that veered away from the main road, the road that the outbound magus had taken. The side road, two ruts with weeds growing in between, curved lazily down to a squatters' village next to the river.

Before reaching it, the corporal left the track and worked his way northward around the village, striking the river two or three klicks downstream from Seldon's nearest border.

Along this stretch of the river, the bottom land was fertile and dotted with squatter's farms, some actively being worked and some deserted.

Avoiding the working farms, he quickly found the one they had told him would be vacant and waiting for him in time of need.

He hobbled his horse and turned it out to graze, then he went down to the riverbank, and, following their instructions, found a wood-framed, leather boat, provisions, and a bundle of civilian clothes in a hidden cache a few meters up from the beach.

He changed into the civilian clothes and launched the boat, which was small enough and light enough for him to drag down to the water's edge.

The whole time he was making his preparations, he kept saying to himself that they had not lied to him, that they had not bungled their end of the deal, that they could be trusted to follow through on their promises, that he would get paid, and that, above and beyond payment, he would get a tiny amount of justice for the decades of evil that Edmund had done to his family!

He hoisted the boat's sail and headed downstream, making his first tack with the wind on his port bow.

He needed to make as much ground as possible on each tack. The current would help. Being able to run the shallow-draft boat well into the shallows before tacking would help. The boat's leeway would hinder. But the wind would decide the outcome as he sawed back and forth across the Columbia River.

Long boards, he prayed. Please, long boards! So and blessed let them be!

Vernon read through the report Bevan had written for him. It was a distillation of the messages that had come in from several different agents, working in several different locations.

It was the stuff of epic poetry. The bards would be clamoring for copies as soon as the word of its availability got out.

An arrow pierced him in the neck.
His plot was now a total wreck.

Brilliant!

Vernon moved on.

Content. He had to focus on the content.

It appeared that Edmund's personal magus had gone hunting: alone, off the Manor Island. He was last observed heading to the northwest on a road that would take him to a junction with another road that would, were he to take it, conduct him onto Fahraq's lands.

It also appeared that Prokoffy, Edmund's commander of the Shore Guard, had captured Ransom. The man was too badly injured to question immediately—that is, to torture with Wolfram's usual gusto—but that was bound to change. In a few days, a week at most, they'd have him begging to spill his guts.

Vernon returned the report to his son and heir. "Find out what the magus is doing. Leave him to do it, but find out."

"I already have it in train."

* * *

Late in the afternoon of Vlod's second day away from the Manor Island, he rode out onto the field where the Brethren had attacked the shore guard.

The crews that Wolfram had left behind had nearly completed the temporary entombment for the ashes of the battle fallen. Piles of debris were burning at intervals across the battlefield.

After speaking with the duty officer, Vlod rode up into the hills, up toward the spot from which the Brethren recall had sounded.

He found the place where Prokoffy had said it would be, a tiny clearing between the ridge line and a steep, treeless drop to the field. The rest was also as Prokoffy had described it. Three horses and four runners had taken up their stations. Behind them in a semi-circle in the trees, a full platoon had acted as guards.

Approach to the three riders had been controlled, though somewhat sloppily.

The four runners may have been eight or twelve individuals, but no fewer than four had been present at any one time.

A single trail led away from the clearing, but it soon merged with a second trail, which within a few meters divided into three separate tracks.

Farther along the ridge line, Vlod found a Brethren staging area, and farther into the trees, he discovered a place where they might have conferred briefly. No fewer than a half dozen trails led away.

Following each of them to its end wasn't possible given Vlod's time constraints, nor was much to be learned by doing so. The tracks would divide and merge and peter out, like game trails.

After making a cursory pass of the battlefield itself, Vlod resigned himself to the futility of his immediate task. Other investigations awaited him.

He obtained a fresh horse from the duty officer and struck inland for Fahraq's.

In the late afternoon, with the sun lowering, Vlod topped the rise above Fahraq's stronghold, and caught the smell of smoke, of charred wood, and of burned and burning human flesh.

As Vlod rode down into the central valley of Fahraq's lands, the odors became stronger, and when he broke out of the trees and into the checker-board of fields, he imagined for a moment that he had blundered into a grass fire. The smoke hung over the fields. It was thick and unmoving and obscured the opposite side of the valley.

In the middle distance, barely visible, a thin column of gray-black smoke rose into the air. At its maximum height, it flattened out and spread over the valley, like batter spreading over a skillet.

At the base of the column were the ruins of Fahraq's stronghold.

Vlod rode across to it in silence, unmolested and, as far as he could tell, unobserved. In the whole of the valley, apart from the dead, he was alone.

The gate towers, which had been constructed of stone and rock, remained. They were scarred but standing. The gates, the curtain walls, and the battlements had been of timber, and they had burned away in most places. However, at intervals, there were undamaged sections.

Vlod hailed the watch, but no one answered.

He dismounted and picked his way over the rubble and across the outer moat, which consisted of an ineffectual dry ditch, and on up into the bailey.

Human and animal corpses, together with the remains of broken carts and wagons, covered the ground. The merchant stalls that had lined the inner perimeter had been reduced to ash. Many of the outbuildings were smoldering or in flames. The crackle and hiss of the fires were the only sounds to be heard.

Vlod spurred his horse on across the inner moat, and up to the inner palisade, the oldest part of the complex. The signs of a hard-fought battle were strewn everywhere: lances, arrows, discarded swords, and more corpses, many of them sprawled in grotesque positions. The fighting had been short and nasty.

The motte proper rose a good ten meters above the bailey, and the palisades an additional five to seven meters above that. The keep, also of stone, rose higher still.

Fahraq and his ancestors had built for nothing if not for height, as though height alone would save them.

It hadn't.

It never did.

The main gate was open, its portcullis lowered but its center smashed. The gatehouse was in flames, the battlements and hoardings blackened or burned away.

Fire had gutted the keep, and the hall had been reduced to a smoking ruin. Here and there, timbers stood like single trees after a forest fire.

Additional corpses littered the area, the spaces between them punctuated with arrows and discarded weaponry.

The victors had left in a hurry; otherwise, they would have taken the spoils of battle with them.

On foot, Vlod climbed to the top of an undamaged portion of the fortress's remaining gate tower. The valley lay spread out below him, and for a giddy moment he imagined that he could grab the rising column of smoke and ascend with it above the carnage, away from the buzz of flies and the squawk of crows and gulls.

Vlod set aside the illusion. He listened for the psychic echoes of victory or the bare relief at having survived. He heard nothing. He found nothing. His senses were blank.

What he was able to touch was a rent in the Harmony, a ragged gap in its fabric that had been caused by the fighting that had taken place.

He noted that despite its size and recent origin, the gap was already closing. The Harmony was healing itself.

Had he been wrong? Had the battle torn the Harmony or had it made it possible for the Harmony to heal?

Physicians amputated arms and legs, cauterized wounds, cut through healthy flesh, destroying the sound in order to heal the diseased or the wounded.

Battles could give life as well as take it.

From where Vlod stood, the dozens of single fires scattered throughout the complex were plain. Their smoke rose separately, but mingled into the gray monolith in the air above him. The suspended ash gritted between his teeth.

Stupidly, he told himself that it was only wood ash and not the ash of burned corpses.

Such was the nature of hope, such was the nature of delusion.

The Columbia River Basin, the Inland Empire and the Holy Oregon, was swimming in such self-inflicted happy talk.

Happy talk or no, human ash or no, Vlod had work to do and he schooled himself to be about it.

Twelve

While Vlod had light to see, he descended the tower and continued his search. The massed voices of the fires rustled like dry leaves blowing across a stone pavement, while the nervous shuffling of his horse, tethered in the inner ward, acted as a counterpoint.

Grace, courage, and style had played no part in creating the destruction around him. But terror had—terror and greed and treason.

He sought the battle's measure. As he did, a further insight formed. It sniggled at the edges of his mind as he studied the valley, the intact fields, the untouched manor henge, the outer and inner wards, the keep, and the walls. It grew insistent as he noted the positions in which the fallen lay, how many of them were in the yards as opposed to on the battlements, the angles the arrows made in the ground and in the walls, the pattern of the fires and their relative ages. One group had burned down to cinders, while the rest were burning as though they were only hours old. At last the insight burst upon him full force.

He cursed his suspicions and his slowness. Prokoffy had not wrought the destruction he was seeing! Prokoffy had not triggered it. *Prokoffy had fought his way out.* He had had an "easy time of it." He had sought to escape, not to destroy.

As Edmund had surmised, and an unknown hand was in play.

Perhaps it had left a trace behind. Perhaps it had *stayed* behind!

He ran to his horse and repeated his search of the complex, but a positive result eluded him.

What he found was not what was there but what there was *not*. No living thing remained in the whole valley, not in the motte and bailey, not in the fields, not in the woods, and not in the barns.

Moreover, he found far fewer bodies and animal carcasses than he should have if the manor had been massacred. There had been heavy fighting, but for the most part, Fahraq's people had left *after* the fighting had decided the issue over which they had fought, whatever that had been.

While he had light to see, he rode to and fro across the valley floor, crossing and re-crossing the roads and the fields, the tracks and the ditches.

One by one, the fires were burning out, and the pall of smoke was thinning. The bite of it eased in his throat.

When it had grown pitch dark, he camped in the inner ward, close beside the wall, up behind the keep. He fed his horse, pulled together a low fire from the smoking remains of a shed, and ate a sparse meal, his back propped against a kitchen garden wall made of brick. His food was cold or burned or both and tasted of smoke or ash or both.

"A few buckets of sand," he observed to his horse, "and we could have ourselves a real picnic."

Later, while Vlod tried to sleep, his horse skittered on its tether, and Vlod pondered the nature and utility of horses as guard animals. Their abilities were dubious, but they did have their merits, if one were a light sleeper, if one's enemy disturbed them or smelled like a predator. After a scant few minutes, he gave up the inquiry.

Whatever the case, whether he was safe, whether his horse would be of any use, he could hardly ride back to the battlefield or to the Manor Island, not without being laughed out of the clan, out of the entire basin.

Some magi kept familiars, animals supposedly as adept in their own ways as their masters were in theirs. Familiars were said to deliver messages, to provide the extra focus, and often the extra jolt of power, required by the magus to perform much of the hidden wisdom, and to act as guard animals.

Vlod had seldom viewed himself as the sort to have a familiar, to form a duality with a psychically powerful animal, but with his horse less than calm, with the night dark and the shadows acting less and less like shadows, with the dead and the stench of death close about him, and with the air crowded by wandering night spirits, he promised himself to reconsider the question.

He contented himself with lighting a single-wicked lamp to blind the wandering night spirits.

Bundled again in his bedroll, he was helpless to prevent his mind from racing. But the racing was without focus, and gradually the horse grew quiet, and the shadows behaved like shadows, and the single-wicked lamp performed its task of blinding the wandering night spirits.

When Vlod had relaxed enough to sleep, his mind slowed into a gentle, focused wandering, and he longed for Brenna's company. He wanted her for herself, for her companionship, but, he confessed to himself, he also wanted her with him for her ability to read a battlefield.

Tremayne might be able to read people, to hear them, but Brenna could read armies! She could hear them even when there was no sound to be heard.

Where Vlod could speculate about the track that the main body of Fahraq's people had taken on their flight away from his keep, she could have picked it out.

He could speculate about the nature of the attack, but she could read the opposing orders of battle by the way the arrows slanted into the ground, by the way the blood had puddled in the dirt.

For himself, on his own, he could spot the traces of Prokoffy's fight to get out of the stronghold, and Vlod could spot the places in which some of the fires had been set: in Fahraq's great hall, at the base of the hall's flanking towers, in the grain store, and in the keep itself.

The fires had been started inside the perimeter of the inner wall. Much of the outer wall was intact, and it was free of the signs of a great deal of fighting, which it would not have been if the main attack had come from *outside* the stronghold.

So the culprits had to have been Fahraq's people acting after his death, or they could have been persons not of his clan lodged within his household, or they could have been a faction that had taken his death to be an opening.

Fahraq dies, a fire is set, there is fighting throughout the stronghold, and the survivors quit the place.

Quit?

Couldn't the victors have taken them away against their wills?

Victors could do as they liked and often did. It was one of the perquisites of victory.

He could trace and he could speculate, but Brenna could have given him the answers he needed by reading the field itself. She could have unlocked its secret history.

Or was he exaggerating?

Perhaps, but she had done more with less.

He fell asleep thinking about her, wanting her next to him in the bedroll, and when he dreamt, it was of a beach in high summer, with the sun lowering toward the ocean, and of her walking up from the waves, backlit and golden.

In the morning, the fires were out, and the ashes that were left sent up spindly trails of white gauze. The wind caught them above the rim of the valley and scattered them.

Vlod circled the outer palisades, moved farther out into the fields and circled them again. He had not made a mistake the day before. No less than four groups had left the stronghold, each travelling in a different direction, each taking one of the trade roads or local farming paths. Based on the condition of the horse dung, the groups had left at roughly the same time.

Vlod concluded that at least one of the trails had to be followed. If the remaining three escaped, so be it. They couldn't, though. Sooner or later they would show up somewhere. They would be recognized buying or selling at a market, working in a field, or hauling nets on a river. People did not vanish like smoke.

The choice of which group to follow was arbitrary. He could discern nothing to help him choose among the alternatives. He took the Dice of Heaven from their pouch, but at the last moment put them away. In the end, he picked the track heading south, for no better reason that it stood a good chance of making his return to Seldon's easier.

An hour after leaving the valley, Vlod came to the body of a man-at-arms lying off to one side of the track. Face up, he was in guard's uniform. The tunic was soaked with blood, and the head of an arrow was protruding from the left shoulder. Having no need or reason to investigate, Vlod rode by without dismounting.

In succession, he found a second, a third, and a fourth body, the carcass of a horse, one of an ox, and a wagon with a broken axle.

Early in the afternoon, he found Desmond, one of the magi who'd helped him build the cannon, but who had gone on to betray the project. He was sitting against a tree on a rise above the trail. He appeared to be both sleeping and feverish.

Vlod knelt beside him and touched his brow. It was hot.

Several months ago, the Academy had attached Desmond to Fahraq's House, granting the appointment as a last chance of sorts.

Desmond opened his eyes. They were glassy, and the whites were pink, the pupils dilated. "Don't touch me, you little bastard," Desmond said. His voice was strong, but his breath was foul. He made to pull away, but his strength failed him.

Vlod's hatred for the man evaporated. "I'm no bastard," Vlod said. "I have the certificates to prove that my mother and father were married."

"Says you!"

Desmond closed his eyes.

Vlod tugged at the ties closing the man's cloak. "Let's have a look."

Desmond tried to pull away again, but met with no greater success than before. "Leave it!"

"What happened?"

"Ask Prokoffy!" Desmond heaved himself forward a centimeter or two. "Ask your precious Edmund!"

"They didn't have anything to do with what happened here," Vlod said.

"Bunk!"

"No, I meant, what happened to you?"

"Oh." Desmond let himself fall back. "Slow poison. Harborton's Oil, to be exact. An old score settled. I lose."

Vlod had no difficulty envisioning what might have happened. Desmond was a conceited, angry drunk. He was also cowardly and abrasive. Into the bargain, he had the sexual continence of a stag in full rut. Women, men, it made no difference to him as long as they were willing to fulfill one or another of his urges.

Vlod said, "You racked up an old score in a matter of months? How?"

"Mine wasn't the only one. A lot of old scores were settled."

"A score about…?"

"Your fucking cannon," Desmond said. "They blamed me for it." He paused for a time, but then said, "They may be right. I helped you build the damn thing."

"They're panicking."

"The whole bloody basin is panicking," Desmond said. "They're scared shitless that you'll build another one, or that somebody will. I can't blame them. If Edmund has a cannon and they don't, they're royally fucked. Sideways."

Veering away from the cannon, Vlod asked, "Are you in pain?"

"Tolerably. They stole my medicines."

"You were a popular fellow, weren't you?"

"Heresy leaves a stain." Desmond shook his head. "Sorry. Bad subject."

"No offense taken," Vlod said. "I barely escaped with my life."

"I heard as much. Ulricka plays for keeps."

"That she does."

Vlod opened his kit and mixed an analgesic. When it came to Harborton's Oil, no antidote existed.

"I passed a lot of people on the road." Vlod held the cup out to Desmond, who accepted it with trembling hands and gratefully drained it.

As though there had been no interruption in their conversation, Desmond said, "Most of them dead, unless I'm wrong."

"Every last one of them."

They waited together in silence for a few minutes while the drugs were absorbed into Desmond's blood stream.

Eventually, he went limp against the tree. "How much opium did you throw in?"

"A lot."

"Good of you to be so precise."

"You're in no position to complain," Vlod said. He felt a pang of shame at his words. They were callously flippant. Desmond was dying, and although Vlod disliked him, his death was not something that Vlod would have wished or sought or that he welcomed, not in the cold light of day.

Desmond asked, "Why did Edmund do it?"

"Do what? He attempted to arrest Fahraq for the murder of Dagna's baby."

"We got a different story."

Vlod recounted the murders and the captain's confession.

Desmond said, "She always did impress me as being thicker than the snowpack in January. We were told that Edmund was using the death of his grandson as a pretext to murder Fahraq, and the man did die with one of Prokoffy's arrows through his greasy neck."

"No, it wasn't one of ours."

"Can you be sure?"

"Yes."

"It wasn't just Fahraq, but the whole clan. The clan was gaining strength. Given time, it might have mounted a credible threat."

"Prokoffy didn't set fire to Fahraq's castle."

"No, Lawrence did."

"Your commander of horse?"

"Not mine, Fahraq's. I detested the moronic prick. I wouldn't have permitted him to scrub out the chamber pots."

"What happened?"

"When he saw Prokoffy escape with Fahraq's head in a sack, he wanted to ride down to Seldon's and take revenge."

"Why didn't he?"

"Ransom, the battlemaster, stopped him in the inner ward. They argued and a fight started. I can't tell you how, but it did. It was bloodier than if Wolfram himself had ridden in and hacked the place to pieces."

Wolfram did not hack, he had never hacked, but Vlod shied away from making an issue out of Desmond's choice of words.

Had Wolfram been the one to attack the inner ward, the dead would have outnumbered the living and not the other way around.

"Go on," Vlod said.

"The occasion, as I told you, was used to settle up a number of accounts."

"Let's try again. Who assassinated Fahraq?"

"You won't accept Prokoffy?"

"Take another second guess."

"Lawrence," Desmond said, more or less pulling the name out of the air. "He was the one trying to leave."

"What about Ransom? He was the one who stayed, playing the innocent."

"You'll have to ask him about that. My money is on Lawrence."

Desmond's eyes took on a look of greater distance than before, but it was the work of his memories rather than the effects of the opium or the poison. "That damn cannon. I'd be alive if we hadn't built it."

"We'd be dead if we hadn't."

"How glib you are."

"Sorry, I didn't mean to be. We knew going in that the cannon would be dangerous," Vlod said. "Pick up with the fighting in the inner ward."

Desmond took a few breaths, then said, "When it was over, Ransom had won. Hurray for him! But the fighting had rendered the stronghold indefensible. Ransom is no romantic fool. He ordered the manor evacuated against the chance that Edmund would decide to attack in force."

"Edmund would never have done such a thing! How could Ransom be that idiotic?"

"Was he?"

"Edmund is no murderer."

"You ought to have heard Fahraq's side."

"Strangling commerce? Petty tyranny? Food out of his people's mouths?"

"Something like that."

"It won't wash."

Desmond's eyes were clouded and his breathing showed the first signs of heavy labor. "It doesn't matter," he said. "I'm pretty much beyond caring."

"Me, too."

Vlod gently laid the back of his fingers on Desmond's face. It was warmer than before. The poison was following its course.

Vlod gave Desmond a drink of water, and placed a cool damp cloth across his forehead.

Desmond said, "Stay."

"You've no need to ask. I'll be here."

"I've been a fool."

"Most of us have."

"I don't like the idea of dying as young as I am."

"And if you were older?"

"I could tell myself what a good life I'd had."

"Even if you hadn't?"

"Especially if I hadn't."

They laughed together.

Desmond said, "We've assassinated the Harmony."

"The Harmony is stronger than one little cannon."

"That's where you're wrong. That cannon is like a first cancer cell, like the first show of gangrene, like a dose of Harborton's Oil."

"I hope you're wrong."

"So and blessed let it be," Desmond said. "But I'm not."

———

Desmond died with the setting of the sun.

Using the last of the light, Vlod built the pyre a short distance off the track.

He laid Desmond's body on top of it, and set fire to the driest pieces of kindling.

The wood caught, orange flames sprouted, and as the greener bows ignited, a smoky blaze opened into the night.

Vlod sat on the ground, and cleared his mind. He did not attempt to achieve a particular state of mind. He sought a simpler goal: to experience Desmond's pyre and the night without the confusion of his own rattling mind.

Without trying to, he joined the Mantra of the Two Mountains, and soon his mind was flowing like a placid stream in high summer, without his being consciously aware that it was.

Beneath the alcohol and the anger, Desmond had been a good man, a good magus.

Vlod watched the body burn, and as he did, he heard the inevitable rush of heated air escape from the lungs, sensed the new death lingering in the air above him, warming itself for its journey to the Gods and the Generations.

Below these sounds, and through them, and because of them, Vlod also heard what he could only describe as a silence. It was several meters back in the trees behind him.

The silence was moving. It was circling from Vlod's left to his right, slowly, cautiously, one footstep at a time.

Step, pause; step, pause; step, pause.

The feet slipped, toes first, through the ground cover and caressed the forest floor rather than crushing down upon it.

The step was light; it was a skilled step, a step trained to the ways of silence. It was, therefore, not the step of an animal but that of a watcher. And yet, this watcher was, with equal certainty, no mere watcher. He was young, a double conclusion that Vlod had reached without rational justification. Regardless, it was the step, the approach, the crisp, overly confident weave of a young man.

Vlod watched the flames through half closed eyes and listened.

Time slipped by, the flames consumed the body, the rest of the wood.

The new death departed. Desmond had embarked on his journey to the Gods and the Generations.

The pyre had become an ordinary fire.

The watcher had watched. He did not become a hunter. Interest but not hostility; curiosity but not antipathy; observation but not assassination.

With the fire low, Vlod left the Mantra and checked the hobbles on his horse. Satisfied that the animal would not wander, Vlod added wood to the fire and laid out his bedroll, placing it within the circle of warmth and light, and climbed between the blankets. He drew his battle knife from its scabbard and slipped it under his pillow, at the ready in case he was wrong about his visitor.

The stars above the trees told him that dawn was less than two hours away.

Vlod called into the blackness, "The night is cold. The fire is yours to share if you wish."

No answer. The silence stretching out. Irrevocable. Professional.

"Good night!" Vlod called, and went to sleep.

In the morning, he would either wake up or he wouldn't.

Thirteen

The evening had thickened into night, and the darkness at the edge of the crossroads, away from the torches, enveloped the four riders: Vernon, Mark, Gregory, and a man-at-arms. They all wore dark cloaks without insignia or devices.

In a private ceremony not an hour old, Vernon had changed Gregory's name to Aaronson.

Why Aaronson?

Because Vernon like the way it flowed, and Gregory did not object. In ancient times, a man named Aaron had been a priest and the brother of a prophet. Gregory could do worse than follow in his namesake's footsteps.

Vernon motioned to Mark.

The young officer of Vernon's personal guard beckoned to the man-at-arms, who would be traveling with Gregory, and together they moved off several meters. The man-at-arms was a stolid soldier, a family man, and had served under Gregory's command. Gregory knew him and had approved his choice.

Gregory's horse stirred restlessly, but his second mount and the pack horses remained silent, unconcerned to the point of an ill-tempered indifference.

Gregory shifted in his saddle. "So I'm to leave tonight," he said.

"Yes, you must leave my lands," Vernon said.

"Am I to survive the night?"

It was a fair question, and Vernon could not fault his son for having asked it. "You are, but you must hide yourself. Disappear. You've left Bevan no choice. If he finds you, he'll assassinate you, just as I would be forced to, were you to stay."

"I understand."

"After you attacked him, I ordered him to kill you."

"Father?"

There had been less shock in Gregory's voice than Vernon might have expected. "Let me finish. I thought I could let him do it—for the sake of the clan—but I love you more than life itself, more than him, more than our people. I told him to leave you alone, but he won't."

Vernon and his son were at the junction of four roads. Those that were safe for Gregory to take led to the north, east, and west. Each connected to further roads, which connected to roads that snaked around the compass. His son could choose to travel in any direction he wished, except to return to the manor.

Aaronson was at the start of his new life, one that would be free of armies, courtiers, endless negotiations, and the waste of lives.

"Your brother is afraid of you," Vernon said. "He won't rest until he finds you."

"He won't find me," Aaronson said. "I'll keep moving."

Vernon wondered whether his son was telling him the truth. No one's agents would observe his departure, not Bevan's and not Vernon's. Mark had seen to it, had stationed men to guard against it.

But would such secrecy be enough to ensure his safety?

No. It would only delay Bevan's pursuit, not thwart it.

"It's time," Vernon said. "You should be on your way. Goodbye, my son. May the Gods who Watch guide your ways, and may the Gods and Generations keep you safe."

If Vernon's son went into exile, he had a chance at a new life, and Clan Innis-Martin might have a chance to survive. He had none if he stayed, and the clan would perish.

"Goodbye, Father. May the Gods and the Generations welcome you with celebration."

Leaning in their saddles, they embraced.

Vernon broke away. "After Mark and I have started back to the manor, wait here for a few minutes before departing." Concern flashed across Gregory's face. "You won't be molested and you won't be followed. I don't want to know which way you've gone, that's all. Farewell!"

Vernon wheeled his horse around and dug in his spurs. The animal broke into a gallop.

The road ahead, the road that would guide him back to his manor, was black with shadow. Tears blurred his vision. They overflowed his eyes, and he felt their sting upon his face. He tasted their salt on his mouth.

Now. Now, Gregory was dead and gone, and the chieftain could allow the father to weep.

FOURTEEN

From of its secret place in the desk in her dayroom, Xenia retrieved her unfinished dispatch to the Mother Metropolitan, Ulricka.

Xenia skimmed through to the last page, recapturing the flow of her words. She came to the thought she had left incomplete, and wrote:

I've met privately with Dagna a second time. I invited her to go sturgeon fishing, and she accepted, at her father's insistence, I'm sure. Certainly, she did not accept out of any love for me. Trade and diplomacy will have their due. I repeated our offer, but she did not repeat her flat rejection. The possibilities of what we're offering are working on her resolve.

I beg the Goddess, the God, the Gods, and the Generations that she does. I beg you to pray that she joins her cause to ours.

Dagna has remarkable power. I doubt she's aware of it. To her, it's as normal as the unusual color of her hair. She's always been able to do what she does. She's always had power at her fingertips. She's taken it for granted throughout her life. Often forgotten, always neglected. Her abilities don't enter her head from one day to the next.

The naturally adept tend to be lackadaisical about their abilities. To them, they're nothing out of the ordinary.

I assure you, her powers are extraordinary. I have never experienced the like of it! The merest touch of her mind is like a hammer blow.

To one extent or another, her mother had her trained. The details are in the Cathedral's files. Fortunately for us, the training touched the surface but did not mar her. She remains an uncarved block of marble, waiting to be sculpted.

You've had these comments from me before, but I beg you to heed them. She is highly intelligent, vastly cunning, and strong-willed.

They've treated her like breeding stock, with the result that she is starving for someone or something to love, to which to dedicate her life. This explains her reaction to the deaths of her husband and child: a tormenting, paralyzing grief juxtaposed against a warrior's determination to exact her revenge, preferably by her own hand.

What is truly frightening, however, is the emotion running through the whole of it. This emotion is a searing indifference, not only to the deaths but to her own emotional and physical pain.

Her father and uncle have betrayed her to their grandiose ambitions, and she is bound up in the early stages of realizing it.

She will accept our offer!

Unwittingly, her own father is our best ally. He is our hidden asset, our most telling argument. He will persuade her for us. We need only hold the door open for her. Every year, he grows more overbearing and arrogant. Every year, he grows less and less able to make the sweeping impression of power and invincibility that he did the year before. He is becoming old. Before long, he will be on your knife exactly as Vernon will be on it this year. So and blessed let it be!

Xenia reread what she had written, and satisfied that she had said what she cared to say, she began a new section, the most important in the dispatch.

I'm returning Lyrisette to you. She'll be delivering this note. She's a fine dancer and a good agent, but she's fallen in love with Tremayne, one of my brother's disfavored magi. She did her best to prevent it, and she's hidden it as well as anyone could wish; but her usefulness to me and to you *here* is at an end. (I'm fully aware that you sent her to spy on me. I expect you to place spies in my court. My concern is that they do their work competently. I have nothing to fear from accurate reporting.)

They are very much in love. Tremayne was my lover for a time, as you are doubtless aware, but I harbor no ill will toward either of them, just the opposite.

I would be disappointed if you were to mistreat her because she fell in love.

Xenia paused to consider the last line she had written. Was she overstepping her bounds? Lyrisette was one of Ulricka's dancers and agents, hers to use or to dispose of as she saw fit.

Xenia reread the line several times and decided to leave it in. Ulricka owed her a favor or two. Let Lyrisette's calling and her life be one of them! She had already suffered too much, to use the cliché. To be in love was, alas, to be mistreated.

Raw sex and naked power were much to be preferred.

Like naked breasts. It was stunning how much power they could exert.

Xenia picked up her pen.

As for Tremayne, he is my friend. He is under my absolute protection.

Clear and to spare: a line drawn.

Perhaps the two of them have provided me with another example of why I've come to prefer the sexual companionship of women. With a man, my tendency is to attach.

Invariably, even after the affair is over and done with, I try to hold on to them in some way, as I'm doing now with Tremayne. Women garden; men sow, weed, and reap.

With women, I am free of snares, free to be as I choose. I am able to keep them at an emotional distance and not feel that I am cheating or shortchanging myself. The rules are simple, the exchange conducted at plainly negotiated rates. They are with me for my pleasure, my enjoyment, my gratification, and for no purposes beyond the immediate moment and my immediate interest. My attitude is selfish, but it is also freeing. They do not go without their compensations, the dears.

Why am I burdening you with these self-justifications? I make no apologies for my life, and you have not asked me to do so.

Xenia read back through this last whole section. Would it be wiser to leave it as it is or to recopy the sheet and leave out the lines about her personal life?

Ulricka had no need for the information, and it was impossible for Xenia to believe that the Mother Metropolitan was not fully versed in the details of Xenia's private life.

Would Ulricka take it into her head that Xenia was attempting to seduce her? Doubtful, and of no important consequence if she did. In fact, a liaison in that direction might be useful.

Without question it would be interesting.

Shabnan, the Crone of the Cathedral, would ensure that it was, if not as a participant, then as a procurer.

Choosing to let her words remain as written, she wrote a closing, signed at the bottom, and sealed her message.

The conditions Xenia had set down were not to be flouted. She prayed to the Gods and the Generations that Ulricka and Shabnan understood as much and would not convince themselves otherwise.

FIFTEEN

Sunlight filled Vernon's sitting room, and a late afternoon breeze whispered in through the opened glass doors. The air was fresh and it brought the mud-smell of the river, mud and a faint tang of salt.

Ocean air.

It was as much of the ocean as he was fated to win in his lifetime, before he joined the Gods and the Generations.

He consoled himself with the notion that the faint tang of salt was not the limit of what his clan *might* own.

It was a pleasant idea on a warm afternoon.

His son's face was not pleasant. His heir's expression betrayed the confusion behind his smooth, professional-sounding words, behind his calm phrases and his spontaneous jokes, each of which had been rehearsed countless times.

He had good cause to rehearse, to hold himself in check.

Gregory's baby was dead, but Valeda, the midwife who'd poisoned him, was nowhere to be found...and killed.

Stephania, who'd recruited and controlled her, was alive and in Edmund's custody.

Fahraq, Stephania's father, was dead, but Ransom, his battlemaster, was alive and also enjoying Edmund's hospitality.

Through intermediaries Bevan had gulled Ransom into staging an uprising against his own chieftain. The uprising was to have covered both Fahraq's assassination and Ransom's, just as the attack on Edmund's fleet was to have covered Stephania's escape and Valeda's murder, but the whole scheme was avalanching out of control.

Valeda's supposed murder. Her body had yet to be found.

Like most skilled novices, Bevan had made his work ornate.

Ornate left traces, and Vlod, Edmund's magus, his terrier, was sniffing them out. Soon he would reach the nest.

Vernon did his best to listen to what Bevan was telling him, but the sun was lowering toward late afternoon. The day was as good as spent, and no amount of coffee could dispel the fatigue that was weighing down on him.

Vernon had another distraction. He had seen his son afraid many times before, but from the moment Vernon had begun to instruct him in the ways of governance, not once had Vernon seen him teetering on the crumbling edge of panic...until now.

Gregory would have been the heir by right of first birth but for the Generations. Hatred was a father's due from his second son. The third, fourth, and fifth sons—they seldom cared, or so he'd been told.

He'd had to make due with just the two sons.

His wife, their mother, had died when Bevan was born, and he had chosen not to remarry. Neither had Edmund. Vernon considered that parallel between their two lives, but let go of the thought.

After his wife had died, Vernon had distracted himself with war and concubines, with raids against Edmund and his lackeys, and with plots and whores, and with whores and plots.

He was not being entirely fair to himself. Emlyn had disrupted the routine for a time.

He'd had his sons.

How like a toddler Bevan seemed, seated on the opposite side of the table, waiting for his father to answer, to tell him what to do.

To do.

So often there was nothing to do.

Once more, Vernon was not being entirely fair, neither to his wife, nor to his grief, nor to his capacity to grieve.

Emlyn's loss to him, thanks to a decree by the Geneticists that the two of them could not marry, had struck home. He could not oppose them, nor could he defy them, not without sacrificing his clan.

Neither had it been possible for him to evade the Gods and the Generations. The instant They had made Their pronouncement, his sacrifice of Gregory had been inevitable.

It had been the first of Bevan's many lessons.

The time for his son's next lesson was at hand.

"I cannot tell you what action to take," Vernon said, "or whether any action is warranted."

The child's face lost its color, fumbled its expression of poorly disguised fear.

Staring sullenly, Bevan sipped his brandy. At length, he said, "Vlod—"

Vernon asked, "Who shot the arrow into Fahraq's neck?"

Bevan's eyes hardened for the briefest of instants. "Llewelyn," he said.

"Can he be trusted?"

"I used go-betweens."

"There's a mercy."

"I'm not stupid."

"The mercies abound," Vernon said. "You have a dilemma on your hands. It goes with the blood."

"What would *you* do?"

"Make my own decisions."

With the door to his sitting room closed and bolted, Vernon refilled his glass and went out onto the balcony.

It was a beautiful evening, beyond the reach of Bevan's treachery and cowardice.

Vernon's pain had diminished through the course of the morning, and he had not had recourse to any of the opiates since breakfast.

The manor lay stretched out below him. The smoke from the cooking fires and from his workshops hung over the buildings and the nearer fields.

The manor and the smoke were like a distended pyre. He had burned himself up. He was presiding over his own funeral.

No regrets. No wish to have lived a different life. A rare thing that, among men capable of reflection and willing to undertake it.

The smoke from Fahraq's stronghold would have hung over his lands, filled his valleys, while the bodies of his people had burned.

Vernon didn't have to have been there to know what it had done. It had been a pyre of another sort, for another purpose. Bevan may have lit the fires, but it had not been of his doing. Rather, it had been an accident of Fahraq's own incompetence, of his own inability to rule, to govern: a traitor's pyre!

How well had Fahraq died? Had he thrashed around and pleaded for his life, or had he stood his ground and accepted death with clear eyes and steady hands? Had he had a chance to do either? He wouldn't have had much time.

What had he done when Bevan's messenger had reached him? What were his actions when his own guards had told him that Prokoffy was at the front gate with a troop of men-at-arms?

Vernon sipped the brandy.

He ran it through his mouth, pretending, to himself and for himself, to savor it. He pressed it across the roof of his mouth, and swallowed it, sending it down the back of his throat.

The smoke lowered over the roofs. Perhaps there would be no wind. He would take the boat out regardless. He'd had too few nights on the river.

Too few?

A regret?

No, a comprehension of the cost his life had forced him to pay, had forced those whom he had loved to pay. His wife, Gregory, Bevan: they, also, had had too few evenings on the river.

Emlyn.

He sipped the brandy.

Llewelyn. The name was new.

SIXTEEN

Two days after Vlod's return from Fahraq's lands, Seldon hosted the annual banquet in honor of his ancestor Shillapoo the Great, the builder of the Manor Island's stone curtain walls, the very first walls having been built in wood and brick by Seldon I.

Held on Shillapoo the Great's birthday, the banquet, which was known as the Stone Builder's Birthday Party, drew guests from up and down the river valleys.

The great hall was crowded, overheated, and cramped, with six people sitting where four had sat at the banquet welcoming Edmund, where three could have sat comfortably.

Vlod wished he were somewhere else: in his assigned room up in the Hall, in his cabin aboard *Koan*, at home in his rooms in Olney Castle, in a military encampment, aboard his cutter.

Any of these alternatives would do, but each of them was foreclosed by the demands of his service to Edmund. He considered a mantra, but the stewards were staring at him expectantly, their faces smiling.

Vlod chose the soup, red wine, and a loaf of bread.

The stewards failed to conceal their dismay. They were afraid of being punished by their masters for Vlod's lack of appetite or taste or civility, for his refusal to take part in the banquet, but they were equally afraid of offending a magus. Who could tell what punishment such an offense might bring? The magus himself might forgive them—surely, he might—but would the Gods and the Generations?

Their brows lined, their smiles gone, they placed the dishes before him, bowed, and moved on to attend to whatever needs the next guest might have.

The soup was closer to a thin stew, with too much garlic and pepper. The pepper was greenhouse-grown, rather than imported. Perhaps Seldon was adding another luxury good to his repertoire.

Vlod permitted the sounds of the celebration to swirl around him, to weave into a cocoon of undifferentiated noise.

Paradoxically, he was perfectly alone.

For the first time in hours, for the first time in days, he tried to catch his mind, his consciousness, up to his physical surroundings, to be in his own isolated moment.

No result.

He damned his attempt and its absurdity, and cursed his lack of maturity in the techniques and ways of his calling.

The flow of his thoughts, of his anger with himself, rippled around his feet. He waded out into their main current and let it take him.

Vlod had found and killed his buck, to give credence to the story that he had gone hunting. He'd tied the carcass behind his saddle and rode hard for the Manor Island. He'd arrived, as he had promised Tremayne he would, in ample time for the Stone Builder's Birthday Party.

With the celebration closing in, the kitchens had greedily received the buck.

Vlod had then gone aboard *Koan* and made his report to Edmund.

In turn, Edmund told him that Prokoffy's detachment had been questioned. None of them had killed Fahraq, but one of them had seen the man who'd loosed the arrow. He'd been one of Fahraq's, or at least he'd been in one of their uniforms, but it was impossible to say for certain whether he'd missed a shot at one of Prokoffy's men or had meant to kill his chieftain.

"What about Ransom?" Vlod asked.

"He's well enough," Edmund said. His expression took on a different tone. "I'm afraid his recuperation is at an end."

Edmund called for a torturer, and the three of them rowed across to *Winter Comet,* a large trireme. With just the three of them in the boat, Vlod and the torturer rowed, while Edmund steered.

The captain escorted them to the compartment where they were holding Ransom. As they approached the door, the combined stench of feces, blood, and opened bowels was thick in the stagnant air.

Edmund's jaw muscles flexed, and even in the dim passage, it was easy to see that his face had paled.

The captain was in no better condition. "He was all right a few minutes ago. My executive officer checked on him and reported to me. Every two hours, right around the clock."

"Open it," Edmund said.

"Aye, aye, my lord," the captain said. He slid back the bolt and swung the door open.

They found Ransom inside. He was dead, slumped beside a pile of his intestines, surrounded by a mixed puddle of his blood and urine. He'd used a table knife to disembowel himself.

"How old-fashioned of him," the torturer said. He had gray hair, and liver spots covered the backs of his hands. "I haven't seen a ritual suicides in ages."

Bevan crumpled the note the courier had given him and tossed it into the fire. Ransom was dead, and Edmund, ever the warrior, was charging from position to position in a futile attempt to fill the gaps that were opening in his lines.

Let him!

He was on the verge of learning just how impotent his defenses were.

The Stone Builder's Birthday Party droned on, and Vlod found it impossible to hold himself apart. He changed his ground and allowed the evening to sweep him along, as an observer, not as a participant.

With the meal progressing nicely, it was time for the speakers to play their part. It might have been better if they'd waited until the deserts had been served, but it promised to be a long banquet.

Predictably, the speakers mouthed the proper words about commercial prosperity, industry, and the facilitation of international trade in "a growing community of fraternal cooperation, mutual gain, and unwavering solidarity."

They waxed pious about the pending journey to the Cathedral as a symbol of the clans' united journey into a future of Harmony and faith.

They mouthed the proper sentiments about the courage and ingenuity of Shillapoo the Great, and about the inspiration that his life and accomplishments provided. They were a continuing inspiration to those who lived on the island, traded with it, or who merely passed by the walls he had built.

Seldon had not demurred from, nor had he blushed at, including in his speech two or three of the standard similes about Clan Sauvie being built of individual people just as the Manor Island's curtain walls were built of individual stones. The walls were made of stones, the clan was made of people, and the chieftain, acting on behalf of the Gods and the Generations, was the mortar that held both the stones and the people together. Thus it was the duty of the chieftain to build the stones into walls and to build the people into a united clan. It was the solemn duty and the constant joy of the chieftain to build up Clan Sauvie into a loving family, an entity that was greater than any mere association of families and individuals!

Utter brilliance! Unsurpassed originality! Leadership worthy of Shillapoo the Great, of Seldon I, of Shillapoo the Younger! A comfort and a challenge to everyone who heard it! The true voice of the Gods and the Generations!

The entertainment followed. The first act was a troop of jugglers. They threw flaming batons back and forth, swallowed fire and swords and fiery swords, and kept the requisite number of plates, knives, swords, axes, lances, and people spinning in the air.

The current seating arrangement had thrown Brenna, Tremayne, and Vlod together in the middle of the run of tables on Seldon's side of the hall.

Vlod did his best to pay attention to the conversation bouncing back and forth between them. Tremayne regaled them with his newest find: a jeweler's finger gauge. It was a loop of stout wire onto which had been threaded a large number of standardized "rings," each of which had a number engraved—or possibly stamped—on its surface.

Tremayne demonstrated. He measured each of the fingers on both of their hands, trying rings until he found one that was neither too loose nor too tight. After the third or fourth finger on the first hand, the procedure had gone from interesting to tedious, but he had persisted until the end.

Returning the gauge to its leather pouch, he declared that the three of them had right hands that were larger than their left hands. A decided curiosity.

"We're right-handed," Brenna said.

The conversation moved on, taking up the dangers inherent in digging for artifacts. Many of his finds were considered to be illegal for non-magi to possess, but as a magus and as the curator of the Holbrook Museum, he was largely exempt from those sorts of inane prohibitions.

"Conceivably, that finger gauge could be illegal," Tremayne said.

"Why?" Brenna asked.

"It's made of stainless steel," Tremayne said, using the ancient term for the metal.

"Oh, yes!" she said, as though remembering a long-forgotten lesson. "It won't rust; therefore, it violates the Harmony."

"You're half right. Stainless steel is not a naturally occurring metal, and, therefore, it violates the Harmony."

"Neither is steel, strictly speaking," she said.

"Yes, but steel rusts. Steel uses natural elements to enhance their usefulness; whereas, stainless steel uses natural elements to overcome their inherent properties. Therefore, it won't rust; therefore, it is unnatural; therefore, it violates the Harmony; therefore, it is contraband; therefore, that finger gauge is illegal for me to possess personally."

"You possess it. It's yours to do with as you please, isn't it?" Vlod asked.

"Granted, but it belongs to the museum, so I'm in the clear."

"Look, Tremayne," Brenna said, "white steel—or stainless steel, as you're calling it—isn't the least bit unnatural, nor is it illegal to own."

"In various applications, it is," Tremayne said. "Any number of people are working for an outright, common-sense prohibition."

"Too many things are illegal," Vlod said.

"Like cannons?" Tremayne asked, rather pointedly.

"The jury is still out on that one," Vlod said.

"Not Ulricka's jury."

"Trust me, an appeal is in the works," Vlod said. "It's not mine, but someone is hatching it."

Tremayne made a disgusted face. "Let's hope it's stillborn."

Brenna asked, "All right, genius, explain why bronze is good and white steel suspect."

Tremayne was in his element. He loved nothing better than to explain things, to debate underlying theories.

Vlod found it impossible to listen, and let his mind drift away from the conversation.

Their wrangling would carve out endless semantic circles, but would make no progress toward a solution. Concrete solutions to such arguments didn't exist. They were amusing fantasies.

The endless debates were the one thing that Vlod had loathed about his time at the Academy.

Vlod's focus ranged along the tables, noting the changes in seating from the last banquet. Landis was sitting next to Edmund.

She was bare breasted, as were several more of the women of the court than had been so at the welcoming banquet. For the most part, they were wearing gowns that were variants of the same style: a long, flowing skirt, a tight form fitting waist, and an open bodice that provided support for the wearer's breasts.

The henge and vision dancers were setting the fashion. They carried it well, demonstrating an inherent sense of how to wear it without making themselves overly plain or overly ornate, drab or gaudy, embarrassingly shy or flagrantly overt.

And, like everything else rooted in the Manor Island or in the Cathedral, it was a flagrant style, an immodest style, a demanding style. It asked much of its devotees, including the willingness not to adopt it on the part of those not suited to wear it.

Xenia, who was seated on Brenna's left, had chosen to wear it, and it suited her. Furthermore, she suited it. She had bared her midriff as well as her breasts, but she had added a dancer's veil, a shawl-like garment, which she wore about her shoulder and draped over her left arm. A concession to modesty? A way to emphasize the nakedness of her breasts? With Xenia, anything was possible.

She had, Vlod was disappointed to notice, foregone the snakes coiling around her arms. Perhaps they would have detracted from the veil, compromised the overall spectacle, or perhaps they would have been too much of a bother.

Yes, that had to be it, convenience.

In the strictest terms, Xenia was nearly too old for such attire, especially when compared to the women who had started the craze and to those who had first adopted it, women who were anywhere from five to ten years her junior and who were dancers by calling or who had nothing better to do with their time than to enhance their physical conditioning. Nevertheless, such comparisons aside, she had decidedly not overburdened her looks, nor her character.

And, to interpret the gleam beneath the expression on Xenia's face, she was taking an unrestricted joy in showing herself off, in creating a challenging display, in the pleasure of being naughty.

It was no wonder she had played the role of the "older but not that much older woman" in Tremayne's life.

Equally, it was no wonder that Tremayne kept glancing at her while he was telling them about the perils of archeological digs and museum curation.

The second act was a laborers' guild choir. They sang a medley of time-honored, Manor Island songs: "O Eternal Walls of Stone," "The Bar Maid and the Soldier," "Raise Proudly, Boys, the Sails at Dawn!" "Pretty Abigail," and, at long last, "We Honor Thee O Great Shillapoo, Master Builder of a People."

The choir was not far enough off key to be bad, but it was not on key enough to be good. None of its members would have found success as a *Dirge* singer.

Compounding their crime, the program had been twice as long as it should have been to be effective.

A few hardy cheers, but barely a sprinkle of coin.

The third act was a troop of dancers. Their costumes rendered them more naked than clothed. The men were the products of years of conditioning for attractive bulk and strength, while the women were equally the products years of a no less rigorous conditioning for flexibility, agility, strength, and quickness.

They performed dances that required at least as many of the abilities of acrobats as those of dancers, and they covered the awkward places between routines with an explosion of bare-breasted young women, presumably the understudies, who flitted and cartwheeled and gyrated along the tables.

Arms and torsos rippled, teeth flashed, hair flew, bellies undulated, and breasts bounced—for lack of a better description.

The choreography was sound but mediocre, and the acrobatics were diverting but below professional standard.

Vlod became aware of the deep-voiced bellows before the thick-tongued words intruded into his thoughts.

Their speaker, a man in dress uniform, stepped in front of Vlod, blocking his view of the performance.

The man towered above the table. His eyes were glassy and he was wavering slightly from side to side.

"Magi! Ha! I'll tell you what you are! You're parasites."

"Would you care to repeat that?" Tremayne said, in a hard tone.

"You heard me! You bastards are nothing but parasites."

The man was Fabron. He was one of Seldon's cousins and an officer in his guard. He was taller than most men, and heavier, yet his size was deceptive. He was fast, astute, disciplined, not a man one would expect to be drunk. Tonight, however, he reeked of wine, and a sheen of oily sweat glistened on his blotched face.

Vlod exchanged a nonplussed look with Tremayne, but in exchanging it, Vlod's ignorance shattered and fell away from him, like the clay mold struck from a new bronze. Its place was taken by the necessity before him, by the inevitabilities midwifed by his sense of duty and of curiosity. His trip into Fahraq's lands had touched and the counter strike was about to fall. The weapon of its delivery had just introduced himself.

Brenna straightened in her chair, and her right hand eased into her lap.

"You're drunk, Fabron," Tremayne said. "Return to your place!"

"Hold your tongue, maggot!" Fabron said, rounding toward Vlod. The attack had been general, now it had become specific. "I remember you," he said, as though Vlod ought to have been impressed or frightened, "and I remember the charlatan who is said to have been your father. Heaven knows it couldn't have been him, though. Just look at you. Why, your actual father must have been a runt poodle."

"Fabron! Apologize!" Tremayne said. "You have no excuse for your behavior."

"Indeed not," Vlod said.

"I won't. I refuse." Pointing at Vlod, Fabron said, "His father was the biggest fraud on the river. He should have been roasted years before they finally did it!"

"You will retract those words," Tremayne said, "and you will apologize! At once!"

Vlod stood. "Tre, we're beyond apologies." He loosened the catch on his smallsword. It was a handy weapon, light and fast. It had a razor-sharp, double-edged blade.

The click brought the attention of several in Edmund's clan, but Edmund, Seldon, and Wolfram remained unaware, locked in their conversation.

"Who's going to do your killing for you, maggot?"

"I'll undertake it personally."

Fabron made an open-mouthed show of surprise and mock fear. When he had finished his pantomime of terror, he laughed and moved ponderously into the open space between the rows of tables.

He held up a heavily scarred hand, fingers spread, palm turned toward Vlod. "I've changed my mind! I don't want to find out. You've already told me, but we can forget about that." He made an elaborate show of drying the tears of his laughter from his eyes. "The comedy of it has me weeping like a child. Let me repeat my question. Who's going to do your killing for you?"

"I will," Brenna said. "You have insulted my House. You have insulted my father's magus. You will die for your insolence."

Vlod said, "Take what's left."

Vlod drew his smallsword. The blade caught the torchlight. "The rank is yours, Brenna, but the right is mine. It is a point of personal privilege. Am I not correct, Fabron?"

Seldon's cousin smiled. Arrogance and cunning, bald-faced but deadly, coiled through his mouth and eyes. "Correct you are, fancy talk, and you're as good as dead. First you, and then the bitch!"

Fabron moved farther out into the room.

He drew his sword, and positioned himself with the fire behind him. He rocked slightly on his heels. "Come on, maggot-ette! Don't be shy!"

The noise in the hall hushed to an expectant murmur.

Edmund and Seldon roused themselves from their conversation to find their Houses careening toward a blood feud.

Vlod vaulted across the table. "Brenna, whether I want him or not, this washed-up jackal tripe is mine! He is a gift, sent to dispel the monotony."

His two-edged rapier whistling, Fabron executed an abbreviated form of the waist-circling Tashiyama Kata and slid expertly into the last of the Welt von Eisen forms.

Vlod had to admit that he had done them well, with passion and strength. They had not been the work of a man too far gone with liquor— too far gone with his own ego but not with alcohol.

Vlod inclined his head in a bow of appreciation. "You perform katas expertly."

"They'll serve for you."

Fabron drew his guarding dagger. He gripped the short, heavily reinforced blade in his left hand, the point trained outward. The dagger's quillons were gracefully curved and ornately tipped, fashioned to match the hilt of his rapier.

Fabron grinned disdainfully, and flipped his dagger high above his head. It spun end over end, and dropped snugly back into his waiting hand.

His weapons drawn, his show complete, he stood at his ease, ready to begin, indifferent to whatever danger his opponent might pose. It was an old trick.

Vlod cut the air with his smallsword, limbering his arms and shoulders. He called to the steel, and with each pass, the blade awakened farther from its sleep. Coming awake, it sang eagerly.

The sword was a weapon, not a piece of jewelry. It was plain and strong. It was white fire and summer lightning: it was life and death, summer and winter, skill and courage, storm and calm, humility and honor. It was each of these things, together, at once, given form in the person of a blade forged by the master armorer Matsuri.

Vlod attempted to convince himself that his weapon, a smallsword, smaller and lighter than Fabron's rapier, was no more than inanimate steel, that it belonged to him and not that he belonged to it, and that what he was experiencing was the limbering of his arm, and not the eager quickening of his sword from slumber.

Immediately he grasped the impossibility of the task. With an inner bowing of apology, he discarded his illusions of lifelessness, and accepted the smallsword's possession of him.

Vlod drew his battle knife, and held it as he would a guarding dagger. He prayed that he had neither insulted nor belittled it. In exchange, he felt the handle warm to his touch.

Ever the pupil of Master Yokashima, Vlod abandoned the self and the ego, the desire to live, and the chatter of his mind. He entered into the state of *mushin* and became one with his weapons.

Vlod came on guard in line, his body turned sideways to Fabron, his right foot forward, his blade held a fraction below the level of his shoulders, the point directed at the bridge of Fabron's nose. It was a classic posture, one that Vlod could hold for hours if he chose to.

The time had arrived to await Fabron's pleasure.

In ragged succession, the stewards and wine pourers scurried into the narrow spaces behind the tables.

Fabron circled his rapier, an amateur's tactic. The first worried observations sped from mouth to mouth.

Edmund demanded, "Who gave challenge?"

Vlod did not turn to face his chieftain. Rather, he kept his eyes on his enemy, alert but focused on no single point. He saw the whole of Fabron and the area around him.

Vlod answered, "I did, my lord."

"For what cause?"

"He insulted the dignity of the magi," Vlod said, and had the satisfaction of hearing the breath catch in several throats.

Of his cousin, Seldon asked, "Is this true?"

"They are charlatans. Parasites!" Fabron answered.

"You shall recant!" Seldon commanded.

"With respect, my lord, I will not." The blade stopped circling, and the point leveled at Vlod's heart. "This gutter rat shall die!"

"Fabron, I command you to recant!"

Fabron adjusted his grip on his guarding dagger.

In response, Vlod held his smallsword motionless, preventing it from striking.

Fabron resumed the adolescent circling of his blade. "I may not. Challenge was given and accepted. Am I a coward to hide behind your commands, my lord?"

"Are you a traitor to disobey them?"

"My loyalty is for you to decide, my lord. My honor is for me to defend."

Edmund and Seldon talked together, searching for a means to avoid a feud, a scandal.

Vlod was aware of the timid movements on every side, the panicked conversations, the pompous critiques by the old men of the court, and of the careful scrutiny of Edmund's senior commanders.

Magus or not, was the boy a man? He had often fought beside them many times, but how practiced in their ways was he? A magus, true, but was he one of them? Was he a warrior?

Of the fragments, the ones that lent him the most pleasure, and perhaps the largest advantage, were the frightened whispers about what could happen to those upon whom fell the shadow of an angry magus.

SEVENTEEN

As far as Vlod could tell, Fabron, like most ne'er-do-well men-at-arms, probably believed in this superstition, and the countless others like it. Such a belief could be used.

Very well, so be it. The choice of belief was his. An angry magus casts a long shadow, does he not? Would it extend beyond the length of Fabron's sword, as far as the man who'd paid for its appearance? So and blessed let it be!

An iron calm settled upon Vlod's face.

It was Edmund who spoke for the two Houses.

"Although we will take no pleasure in this duel, it is a point of personal privilege, and, therefore, we may not interfere. However, no matter the outcome, the matter ends here! It ends this night!" He left a silence, time for the import of what he had said to be understood. "May the Gods Who Watch decide!"

"So and blessed!" Seldon added.

It was upon them, Vlod and Fabron, one would live and one would die.

Vlod held his position, declining to attack. Deliberately, he chose the defensive position. "To open with an attack is to surrender to your pride. Be humble. Adopt a posture of unafraid humility," Yokashima had said.

"Moreover, when you attack, you clear the path of your own destruction. Therefore, remain without ego. Your enemy will break, and when he does, stride boldly down the path that he provides."

Vlod quelled his inner mind, and watched Fabron.

But Vlod did not see him. Rather, Vlod saw, without inner comment or critique, the pattern of Fabron's stance, the rhythm of his breathing, the direction of his eyes, and the welling up of his spirit.

A blink, a ragged breath, a muscle twitch, a wavering of resolve, a shift in the pattern of Fabron's stance, a break in his state of mind: any of these could signal the opening of an attack, any of these could provide the path down which Vlod would boldly stride, down which his sword, of its own, would lead him.

Mushin. Or an attitude of mind like it. The warrior is silent within. Seeing directly, he acts directly, without the intermediary of thought. He does the needful, does it in time, does it without the deliberate choice to do it, and does it without the twin fetters of desire and fear.

Suddenly Fabron raised his guarding dagger, circled his sword above his head, and slashed savagely down toward Vlod's neck.

The magus blocked with his battle knife and lunged at the unprotected area below Fabron right arm, the weakness, the inevitable opening, created by the attack.

At the last instant, Fabron's guarding dagger turned aside Vlod's smallsword.

Left unprotected by his extension, Vlod returned to guard, parrying Fabron's riposte as he did so.

A rapid exchange of thrusts and parries followed, and, because he was much smaller than his opponent, Vlod was forced to give ground or be hacked to pieces where he stood.

Vlod stayed his retreat, and the two men met in a wrenching clash.

They separated within seconds, and stared at each other across the tips of their poised weapons.

Fabron's chest was heaving, and trickles of sweat ran down his face and into his beard.

During the exchange, they had circled, and Vlod had ended up facing the head table. Edmund, Seldon, and Prokoffy were watching the duel with studied detachment, and Tremayne, still in his place, was ashen-faced.

Wolfram was in a category of his own.

His face was relaxed, noncommittal, he studied the hall as he would study any battlefield, the disposition of forces, their relative weights.

Wolfram decided that Fabron would give Vlod a good dusting, but that the outcome between them was sure in its own right.

It was, however, unlikely that Fabron would have been so foolish as to launch his attack without support or reserves. He was no amateur, but he didn't have the skill or the courage to attack alone.

Wolfram asked Prokoffy, "How many?"

"Two with one in reserve."

Edmund said, "Guard his back."

Prokoffy left the table and slipped into the dimly lit areas, the unnoticed places along the perimeter.

At his signal, a half dozen of his men-at-arms shifted their positions and limbered their weapons.

Wolfram let his gaze roam about the hall: Prokoffy's men, Seldon's guards, the dancers, the wine pourers. Wine pourers were always good for a bit of treachery. His gaze touched on Brenna. Her face was intent, her eyes slightly narrowed. She was searching, cataloging, judging, placing.

Her right arm disappeared below the level of the table.

In a gesture of fair warning, Brenna set her battle knife on the table in front of her.

Xenia arched an eyebrow.

"If Vlod dies, it will be by Fabron's blade and by no other," Brenna said. She turned up the corners of her mouth in a parody of the feminine sweetness affected by the majority of the Manor Island's women.

"You insult the honor of my brother's court!"

"Oh? Then it was your brother's *court* that arranged for Fabron's attack on my father's magus?"

"I protest!"

"Xenia, my dear, I do beg your pardon. It would be impossible for me to insult the honor of your brother's court."

Fabron was on the move. He circled to the right, reversed himself and circled to the left, ending where he had begun, as though he were being guided by an unseen hand.

"You insult us!" Xenia said.

"Would you care to wager on the proposition?" Brenna asked.

"Honor is not a matter for gambling," Xenia said.

"Truly? How is it then that you, Xenia, are so perilously close to wagering your life on it."

"I haven't challenged you."

"I didn't say you had. Assassination is your line of country."

Xenia's face paled.

"A women's duel perhaps?" Brenna asked. "Guarded blades and guarded faces? No, thank you. Challenge me and the game is for real."

Xenia began a retort, but Brenna waved her to silence. Her attention was better spent in guarding Vlod's back.

Fabron retreated a half pace, attempting to draw Vlod forward, to overextend.

Brenna was proud to see that Vlod held his ground.

He was leaving Fabron to be overextended, to be outdistanced by his own attempt at cunning.

Fabron shifted his balance to his rear foot, his nostrils flared, and on his exhale, he stepped forward, his sword flashing into the opening arc of the Sixth Coin.

Fabron's technique was exact, filled with power, determination, and an uncompromising will to victory.

Doubtless, he was performing the technique exactly as his instructor had taught it to him, as he had chosen to learn it: as a sequence of smaller techniques: first this, then this, then this, followed by this.

At the same time, it was unfair to blame Fabron's barbarism on his instructor. A sensei can only teach. It is the student who must learn, who decides when the lessons are finished. No master, no sensei, would refuse a willing pupil, would be uncandid or dissemble without a reason.

Vlod wondered whether he were witnessing Fabron's master's just cause: a stylish *performance*, complete with indications of mental acuity and vitality of spirit, but it *was* a performance and not an attack!

Fabron's blade was sweeping toward Vlod's shoulder, but he disregarded it.

Master Yokashima would have cuffed any of his students who had dared to offer him—or themselves!—a display such as the one Fabron was putting on.

The sweep of Fabron's sword had nearly finished when Vlod's sword and his body gave answer. His sword parried, while his body rolled away from the attack, feigning desperation in the face of certain death.

No sooner had Vlod done so, no sooner had his actions beguiled Fabron away from the Sixth Coin, than Vlod's sword counterattacked. A thing possessed of itself, it lunged toward Fabron's chest.

Fabron was not without reflexes, and met the thrust with one of his own.

With a violent check, their weapons locked, corps-a-corps, and for a sickening moment, the duel became a wrestling match.

Fabron bore his weight down onto their crossed blades, and Vlod had no choice but to brace against the onslaught of the man's weight.

Incredibly, Fabron's advance halted, and an opening presented itself.

Advancing into it, Vlod brought his battle knife into attack position, but at the same time, he caught himself calculating the thrust instead of making it. And in that instant, in that thinnest slice of consciousness before he could clear his mind and rejoin the flow of combat, Fabron parried with his guarding dagger.

For an insane instant, their weapons seemed to shriek in pain under the shock.

A snap like the sound of breaking bone lashed Vlod's hearing, and the resistance he had been facing vanished. His body lurched forward, and Vlod found himself in danger of stumbling headlong onto Fabron's dagger.

The man's rapier had broken!

Vlod checked his fall, and simultaneously the broken section of Fabron's sword clattered onto the floor.

No longer falling, but in an impossible position, Vlod twisted away, parrying Fabron's attempt to stab him with the stub of his sword.

Ending on the floor, Vlod rolled and vaulted onto his feet. In a continuous, fluid movement, Vlod returned to his on-guard position.

Fabron threw the useless hilt of his rapier aside. He shifted his guarding dagger from his left to his right hand, and crouched into a knife-fighting stance.

Mocking Vlod's skills, Fabron tossed his dagger from hand to hand. The blade reflected the light from the torches.

The first traces of fear nipped at the heels of Vlod's resolve. In Fabron's eyes, he saw an image of his own pyre, and the desire to run from it beckoned to him.

He saw the ugliness of his fear, saw its source, held it within his heart, and then renounced it. He would not betray himself, nor Edmund's clan, nor the Matsuri blade he wielded, nor the teachings of Master Yokashima.

Vlod had lost his state of *mushin*, and he had but one hope: to step forward!

Vlod called to the hall at large, "Sword! A sword for my opponent!"

A moment later, a blade clattered at Fabron's feet.

He stooped carefully, never taking his eyes from Vlod, and picked it up. He tested the balance, cut it through the air a few times, and came on guard.

Vlod cleared his mind and became again one with his weapons. He stepped into the Way and regained the warrior within.

And in the midst of this inner wordless calm, a thought formed. The nape of his neck prickled, and he gave the thought its head. The flitting dagger, the testing of the replacement blade, and Fabron's smooth self-confidence could have but one meaning. The show was not the attack. Vlod wasn't fighting a duel, he was participating in his own assassination.

Vlod circled to the right, scanning the hall. He searched the tables and the faces of Seldon's comfortable, self-indulgent burghers. The faces that stared at him were nothing if not expectant. They were the faces of men and women who were smugly elevated, morbidly fascinated, but when the day was done and the blood had soaked into the ground, their concern would be at an end.

The faces Vlod saw were the faces of people who were preoccupied with their private anticipations of the entertainment, of the positively thrilling diversion from their self-constructed, self-imposed boredom, to be gained from a duel to the death.

So long as the outcome would be a death, they were indifferent as to which of the duelists would die. What was one magus more or less as long as someone else killed him? A man-at-arms, one of Seldon's cousins? That loss would excite no worried comment. The woods were full of Seldon's cousins...and of his bastard sons. The cause? The outcome? Who cared? A man's death, a real death was about to entertain them!

Fabron's treachery was preferable.

It took no great skill for Vlod to pick out the dandy who was to be his executioner. He was of medium build and sported the face of a pampered woman, a woman of the court. Within the dictates of anonymity, he was moving cautiously along the rows of tables, holding to the half-lit places, the dim alcoves. He was doing his best to keep himself within Fabron's line of vision, which meant that he was watching Fabron and not Vlod.

A second dandy was following the first. Had the room been a circle, he would have been ninety degrees behind. He was moving as the first did, out of the direct light. His marks were his blond hair and his red-and-yellow jacket, cut short and trimmed with fur that had been died sky blue.

Ah, Yokashima-san, they build not paths but highways!

On the other side of the coin, there were two of them, and having a route along which to attack and being able to mount an attack along it were two quite different things.

Vlod might be able to deal with the one, but the second was a problem of a different sort. Vlod might drop the one, then dance away from both Fabron and the second's knife, but—

Enough!

The event would take care of itself! His weapons would do what was needed. He banished his thoughts, his internal dialog and pointless debate.

The words came to a stop, his breathing slowed, and his eyes saw what was before them.

An exchange of thrusts, jabs, parries, and ripostes came and went, and as the two men drew apart, Vlod changed his grip on his battle knife as if to shift it into stabbing position.

Fabron's smile widened, and he nodded with only slight perceptibility.

In one action, devoid of calculation and deliberation, Vlod lunged at Fabron, and, pivoting his head, reversed his line of sight. The first fop was just to the left of where he had expected him to be, his dagger raised, hesitant while he consumed a precious fraction of a second: first, to comprehend and, second, to aim.

Such luxuries were ill-afforded!

Vlod's battle knife struck hilt-deep into the first assassin's neck.

The man's eyes bulged. He made a wet, rasping gurgle, and collapsed forward across the table behind which he had been standing, falling face down, amid the screams of the women of Seldon's court. His blood had spurted onto them, spoiling their new gowns and leaving their faces and their naked breasts flecked with red.

The assassins' throwing knife clattered onto the floor. The handle was wood, the blade plain—an anonymous weapon, common and untraceable.

Extended in a lunge, Vlod tumbled away from his line, away from Fabron's counterattack, and faced the second assassin.

The man's knife was already in the air.

It passed over Vlod, missing by centimeters.

It struck the wall of a fire pit, bounced off, and rattled across the floor.

The first assassin had yet to die. He clutched at the ivory handle of Vlod's battle knife. He rolled over onto his back, choking on his own blood. He kicked and flailed and squirmed like a worm being threaded onto a fishing hook.

The men and women of Seldon's court shrank away, shrank away as they would from an overturned cart of shit.

Finally, the body stiffened, jerked twice, a third time, and lay motionless. The fop's dead eyes gaped in frozen horror up into the face of a wildly screaming woman. Blood-spattered, hysterical, clothed in jewels and silk, she was the wife of one of Seldon's grain merchants.

The body slipped from the table and collapsed onto the floor.

Brenna was on her feet. Her battle knife was in her right hand, held cocked above her shoulder. Her left arm was extended, a rod targeting the second henchman. She was poised between condemnation and execution, held in the instant by the gathering of her power, blind to no concern save the honor of battle.

Fabron withdrew beyond the reach of Vlod's blade. His fear was evident, his desire to run was written in his stance, but the game was set, and Vlod had left him no choice but to play it out. Fabron realigned his dagger and his borrowed sword, and jabbed toward the outside of Vlod's right shoulder.

Vlod parried and gave ground.

The second henchman drew a second knife from his sleeve.

The point of it hadn't cleared his cuff before Brenna had released her own. The throw was true, and for the half second it took for the blade to reach its target, Brenna held the final position of the technique.

She was alive, marvelously and completely alive. Her every nerve, every muscle, every bone burned with the searing strength of that life. For her, neither past nor future existed. The moment, the instant in which she lived, was the sum and whole of her existence. She was death and life and honor: she was indictment, and she was judgment. She was justice. She was Warrior!

The henchman's scream restored the world of things and the rush of time. He fell against a brazier, sending it over in a shower of burning coals, cinders, and smoke. He followed it onto the floor.

Further numbers of the court scattered, yelling oaths and curses, one with his jacket on fire. Writhing against the wall, he beat at the flames with his hands.

The fire from the brazier caught a tapestry and the flames shot up. Amid screams and shouted orders, the nearest men-at-arms tore the woven mural from the wall and crushed out the fire, while a steward used a jar of Seldon's best wine to extinguish the burning jacket.

The man's panicked cries faded to anguished whimpers.

To his credit, Seldon sat at his table, mute.

Vlod planted his rear foot, and blocked Fabron's latest riposte.

The two underlings were dead: the end of the game was at hand.

Vlod's block reformed into a shortened attack, which was turned aside.

The two men moved apart.

Fabron was breathing heavily, and a thick film of sweat covered his hands. He was nearly spent.

Vlod eased into a reverse stance. His right hand held the grip normally, but his left grasped the blade just ahead of the guard. Here Matsuri had built up a smooth section with small hand stops for just such a purpose.

At rest within himself, neither attacking nor defending, Vlod held his stance.

The coals that had spilled from the brazier were being cleared away, the courtiers were returning to their places, and Brenna was receiving a replacement battle knife from one of Prokoffy's men-at-arms.

Fabron lunged.

Vlod's blade swept forward in a wide arc, throwing Fabron's blade out of the way. Simultaneously, Vlod stepped forward through the sweep, finishing with his left foot forward and his sword close to his right side.

Fabron stumbled in retreat, and Vlod double-lunged, releasing the blade from his left, and throwing his right foot far forward while at the same time extending his right arm in a deep lunge aimed at Fabron's heart.

But the tip of his sword finished its flight in empty air.

Fabron had wheeled away, out of range, scrabbling to regain his balance and to build a defense.

Let him! He was well beyond the limits of his power to help himself.

The draw and rush of Brenna's substitute battle knife touched Vlod's awareness. A third henchman?

Vlod was off his game: he had counted only two!

Beyond Fabron, the third assassin cried out.

Brenna was on her feet. Her substitute knife was buried up to its hilt in the third assassin's chest, while a blood-red froth fountained from his mouth. He reeled against the wall behind him, and slid down onto the floor. There, he moaned once and died.

The third assassin's throwing knife was lodged in the back of Brenna's chair. She pulled it out, and casually dropped it in front of Xenia. "A memento of the honor of your brother's court."

Xenia's shock may have been real, or it may have been well-acted. "Thank you," she said, "but you must keep it. Never fear, though, I'll be happy to pass along your message."

In Fabron's eyes, where challenge and fear had been, there were now hatred, and loathing, and the awareness that his life was ending.

Vlod, ever mindful of the obligations of honor and of his being as a magus, performed the kata of the Weeping Victor, and spun the Death Wheel.

His blade circled before him, gaining speed; and as it did, it transformed into a murderous blur. A distinct, living presence, alive in and of itself, it hovered in the space between him and Fabron.

Transcendent of any braggart's secret thrust, of Fabron's self-consuming sword-work, the Death Wheel was the special discovery of the downriver magi. Their own hidden knowledge, it had been among the last things taught to him by Master Yokashima.

"A circle contains each of the directions in which a man can walk," Yokashima had said, his accent flavoring the mystery, deepening its importance. "In this same way, the Wheel contains each of the paths in which a sword may travel to an appointment."

"What is the defense?"

Yokashima grinned merrily. "To spin a Death Wheel of your own."

Fabron was in no position to spin a Death Wheel of his own, if he could have. Rather, he feinted to the left, and Vlod lunged.

Vlod's smallsword caught Fabron's rapier and flicked it from his hand. The steel cartwheeled onto the floor, bounced, and slid under a table.

With his dagger, Fabron pushed the blade of Vlod's sword away, but Vlod's attack was not to be thwarted with such untutored ease.

Vlod pressed his blade to Fabron's, and, as though welded to the spot of contact, followed it through the maze of gyrations that Fabron used in a desperate effort to shake it loose.

Finally the dagger was torn from Fabron's hand.

The steel sailed across the room.

The end was at hand!

Vlod advanced, his sword leveled, expecting his opponent to flee; but in the face of his own mortality, Fabron turned out to be no coward. He did not run, nor did he ridicule Vlod's victory, nor did he plead for his life.

Vlod thought of Seldon's pampered burghers. Fabron deserved better than to die for their entertainment.

Vlod pressed the point of his sword into Fabron's cheek, opening a deep cut. A stream of blood erupted and ran down the side of Fabron's face and across his beard.

"Keep your life," Vlod said. "Magi do not murder."

Without speaking, Fabron bowed and strode evenly toward the doors.

Watching him depart, Vlod wondered if he had seen the last of Fabron and his garrulous gang of cheery cutthroats.

EIGHTEEN

With the dead cleared away, like a dish that had not pleased, the Stone Builder's Birthday Party was closing in on its conclusion.

A final troop of acrobats were performing in the center of the hall. They built human structures that towered into the rafters. One after another, the structures collapsed in showers of tumbling, spinning humanity, only to reform in subsequent patterns of increasing improbability.

In a lull between routines, Brenna handed Vlod the dagger she had pulled from her chair. "White steel."

Tremayne leaned into the conversation. "White steel? I've heard about new supplies. May I see it?"

Vlod passed him the dagger. "What have you heard?"

"A lot of nonsense." He held the weapon in one hand, resting the flat of the point on the heal of his other hand. "But maybe not." He tipped the knife back and forth, causing the torchlight to play across it, to reflect off the facets of the blade. "Remarkable. Extraordinarily light. Good balance."

"A fine piece of work," Brenna said.

Tremayne examined the blade, millimeter by millimeter. "Either it was recently forged, which is impossible, or it was taken, or sold, from an unregistered cache, which is equally impossible." He handed it back to Brenna. "Would you be willing to part with it?"

"Sorry, Tre. A girl has to have some treasures, doesn't she?"

"Oh, well, it deserves better than sitting in a display case."

"It does indeed," she said. and slipped the knife into her belt.

With the image of the dagger fixed in his memory, Vlod guided the conversation away from it and away from the subject of white steel.

He'd had sufficient danger for one night.

NINETEEN

After formally closing the banquet, Seldon invited his sister into his private study.

To his surprise, she agreed to join him without protest. It *was* unusual of her. In a weak moment, he might have called her acceptance gracious; but he was determined to have no weak moments, no lapses into familial good feeling. For that reason, among others, he interpreted her action as prima facie evidence that she had a demand of her own to make.

His invitation hadn't allowed her to change clothes, and as a result she was still in her court dress—or out of it, depending on how one considered the question.

When he ushered her into his book-lined sanctuary, rather than use her veil to cover up, she lay it across the coat stand.

She went to the fireplace, and tossed a couple of pieces of wood into the flames. Then she sat in the chair she normally occupied when she visited him in his study, and stretched her feet out toward the hearth.

"I've always loved this room," she said, settling in.

"Coffee?"

"Tea. Are you making it?"

"I'm not helpless," he said, swinging the kettle over the flames.

"I wasn't offering. You make better tea than I do. That's all."

He set out the cups, saucers, the tea pot, and the rest of the kit. He'd ordered his steward to send the water up from the kitchens already hot. Seldon had only to bring it to the boil.

He was no prude, but why had she exposed her breasts? Why had she worn that type of gown to the Stone Builder's Birthday Party? She had to have known that he'd object, that he wouldn't permit her to repeat the performance.

Wouldn't permit?

Now there was a cruel joke. Her chieftain or not, he had no such power, either to permit or to forbid.

The best he could hope for was that if he did object, his objection would tone down the worst of her behavior for a time.

I've been exposing them for months. Why shouldn't I? The henge dancers are doing it!

You're not a henge dancer!

A lot of other people, too.

You're not a lot of other people. You're you.

And you're you, and I've seen you stuffing prick-shaped padding into your trousers.

Draw.

"Did you enjoy the Builder's Party?" he asked, mildly.

"One of your better efforts."

"One of yours, too."

"Thank you," she said. "I really did put myself out."

"I noticed," he said, refusing to laugh at her joke or to take it up with a rejoinder. Veering away, he said, "For a while, I thought you were going to challenge Brenna to a duel."

"I nearly did, but I have my quota of dueling scars."

He laughed. "Scars? Xenia, she wouldn't have let you off with a nick or two."

"A nick or two is all I'm willing to risk, for the time being."

Her explanation sent a shudder through him. What was she telling him?

Seldon, as he often did with his sister, felt out of his depth, far from shore and floundering.

Like many of the women in his court, Xenia *played* at fencing. True, she had fought several duels, but always with guarded blades and face masks, and, yes, she was fairly good with a sword, but she was no warrior, no duelist!

Brenna was a duelist. And Dagna. And Vlod. Seldon was willing to bet a year's profits that if anyone could find a guarded blade in that household it would be because he'd smuggled it in there himself!

"Been practicing, have you?"

"Maybe," she said. "It won't happen, though. You wouldn't want me to pick a fight and then kill her for sport, would you?"

"No, not for sport," he said, trading her sarcasm for sarcasm. "Wait until there's a good margin to be had, and then do it."

She laughed. "How like you, you are."

"I can hardly be like anyone else, can I?"

The water came to the boil.

While he made their tea, Seldon attempted to consider his sister objectively. If she were an enemy, which in a sense she was, what would he expect his battlemaster to tell him about her?

To begin with, she was a handsome woman in her very early thirties. She was not classically beautiful, but she was a striking, thoroughly desirable woman—and she knew it.

At this point, Seldon had to admit that if she weren't his sister, he'd be tempted to bed her, despite her usual preference for girls.

She had thick, flowing hair. It was brown with red highlights. She had bright, cold eyes. They were brown, and to called them cold, as he just had, was an understatement.

Her breasts were large and perfectly shaped, and had dark, well-defined nipples. They were obviously worth the effort she'd taken to show them off. Most of the men in the court—and no few of the women—had stared at her tits, off and on, the whole evening.

He finished making their tea and poured it, sweet and strong. He had business with her, important business, matters of state, not another one of their wrangling matches about the supposed rights of the Pool of Eileen.

But the importance of his question notwithstanding, with the two imported china cups sitting on the table between them, with a comfortable fire burning on the hearth before them, warming their feet—and her breasts, for pity's sake!—he couldn't settle on an approach.

When it came to his sister, approach was everything: the whole of the bloody game. Oddly enough, that was precisely the matter at hand: "bloody game." Human blood: a real-life outcome.

While they chatted on about banalities, he drank his tea, one sip at a time.

He ought to have planned this encounter out well ahead of time, prepared his interview, but he had not thought to do it until the last moment, when they were already leaving the hall. The urgency of the thing had sprung upon him like a mountain lion springing from an overhanging ledge.

He refilled their cups. He had counted on the tea to disburse the post-banquet fog obscuring his mind, but either the fog was refusing to clear, or he had made the tea too weak.

Unable to choose, he chose to continue with banalities. Gesturing at her breasts, he said, "I don't approve."

"I'm sorry you don't like them," she said, in mock regret. "I'm told I have nice breasts. They're supposed to be haunting, pert, well formed, and a lot of other flattering things. Welford told me they were quite smart. He went so far as to say that they were remarkably outstanding. Hahaha! Ethan said I had the loveliest nipples in the hall and that he hoped to see more of them. He offered me his brand-new slave girl (she is a comely little thing!) in exchange for just one good suck! Each!"

"Oh, give it a holiday," Seldon said. "I was talking about your dress."

"You don't approve of open bodices?" she asked, feigning confusion. "They're the new style. Have been for over a year. You told me yourself that I ought to keep up, and I don't droop at all." She arched her back and twisted from side to side. "See? No sagging. Not a bit."

"Stop it! I don't approve of *your* open bodice. It's unseemly. You're not a dancer and you're not a whore! You're the sister of a chieftain."

"Well, Lord Seldon, since my naked breasts upset you so much, I think I'll keep them naked from now on. Rain or shine, hot or cold, year in and year out, whether the fashion changes or not, my breasts will bask in their nakedness and in your priggish discomfort...until they start to droop, that is, or turn ugly. Then I'll cover them up again and be a proper, provincial matron for you and your proper, provincial court of old women."

"You *are* a bitch," he said, as though he were reaching that conclusion for the first time, which he wasn't. "A real bitch!"

Leaning forward, her arms braced on her knees, Xenia looked over at him. She grinned, a young, happy grin. "I glory in every minute of it! So be damned to your propriety and to hell with your fucking court!"

The firelight caught her face. It gouged out hollows where none had been before. At thirty-two, she was growing old, and if she was, then at forty, so was he. He had no need of the slanting light of a fire to reveal it to him.

Together, brother and sister, they were running out of time, running out of life. Their grandparents had run out. Their parents had run out. Their aunts and uncles had run out. Various unlucky cousins.

Early middle age, middle age, old age, and then death. He thought of his sons, but her touch and her words stayed him, restored him to the present, forced him to attend to his task.

She had reached across and touched his knee. "There!" she was saying. "I've had my fun at your expense. Your devoted and loyal sister is at your service. What have your spies told you that I'm up to?"

Was she trying to make it easy for him, or was she laying a trap? Why hadn't she left him to flounder? She always did, and he always did. A conversation between them would be incomplete without it. Why that particular, helpful opening?

He didn't have time to find the answers. They would have to wait.

He sipped his tea and set the cup in its saucer. "The problem with being middle-aged is that one is neither old nor young," he said. "One is afflicted with the first earnests of the physical infirmities of age, yet one has none of the wisdom, none of the freedom, none of the license to indulge eccentricity, and none of the perspective of age." He put a verbal point on *perspective.*

She had one perspective, while he had another. She had to agree that his perspective as chieftain must take precedence ahead of hers. Didn't she?

He answered his own question, filling for himself the silence that she was allowing by not speaking.

As with everything else, no, she did not! She never had, and any hope that she might agree to at this juncture was a leftover fantasy of his childhood, of his first two or three years as chieftain, a period during which she had indulged her brother. Long ago. Long, long ago. Before she had involved herself in the secret lives of the Cathedral and of Eileen's Temple.

"Nor is one young," he said. "One has none of the heedless energy and untrammeled self-confidence of youth, none of its spontaneous joy. When middle-aged, one is too old to be a fool and too young to be wise."

"What treason am I expected to confess?"

"What treason have you committed?"

"Would I tell you if I had?"

"If I wanted you to, you would."

He let the implication hover in the air above their teacups.

Through the years, he had ignored too many of her political and religious dalliances, too many of her ideological infatuations. She had woven together this and that: a plot here, a strategic marriage there, an assassination in another place. Nothing had been directed specifically or openly at him or at the interests of their clan. She was careful in that regard, and because of it, he had countered and checked her moves at a distance, stealthily, with political and military gentleness, with a light hand, and with lots and lots of money.

She had mistaken his discretion for weakness.

In and of itself this was a bad thing. Misunderstandings between adversaries always were. They couldn't be otherwise.

The time to disabuse her of her misapprehensions was busily insinuating itself upon them and into the life of their clan.

One of the pillars that held up their world was dying, and the other one was, to use the phrase, distracted, weakened by his personal losses.

"Am I meant to tremble?" she asked.

"Two days from now, when our heads are clearer, I shall call in my best spies and tell them to find out who gained control of Fabron and how it was done. I shall not be particularly squeamish about their methods nor about their choice of those to whom they are applied."

"I take it you mean that I am," she said. "You took the long way around, but you're being remarkably clear."

He refused the challenge. "If you're controlling Fabron, I want to hear it from you before I hear it from them."

"Am I to answer you tonight, or am I to answer you tomorrow morning? How about a couple of days from now, before you call in your fingernail rippers?"

"Will the truth change before morning?"

"The truth changes constantly," she said. "Why couldn't Fabron have acted on his own? He is a bully, and he does hate the magi."

Seldon made a disbelieving face at his sister. She couldn't possibly believe such drivel. What made it worse was that she might imagine that he was so stupid as to believe it himself. "Because he couldn't have."

"Why not? They flunked him out of the Academy. He hates them passionately."

"Hatred is not skill."

Xenia shrugged. "Very well, but it is not I, nor is it any of my people." She refilled her cup. "Not any that I know of." Setting the pot back on its hearth stand, she said, "You should have done it, though."

What a surprising turn! Following it, he asked, "Why kill a junior magus?"

She stared at him, hard. The expression in her eyes was twin to the one that he had seen dozing in the eyes of her house snake, an enormous Malheur cobra.

"Edmund does not collect magi the way you do," she said. "You collect trinkets, concubines, and magi." Her generosity in condescending to explain Edmund's statecraft to her less mentally facile brother was blatant in her voice. What was more, she was making no attempt to disguise it. "He has four important magi: Royden, who sees to his technology and business affairs; Aerian, who sees to technology directly for Edmund; Warrick, who sees to his clan's marriages and babies; and Vlod, who reports to Edmund and who sees to everything else. Of the four, Vlod is the one who's a danger to you. He is fiercely intelligent and he is loyal unto death and beyond. Defeat Vlod, and you defeat Edmund."

"Dozens of people want to defeat Edmund."

"Yes, but dozens can't," she said. "An assassin can. Hence, Fabron's attempt on Vlod's life. It might or might not have been the first. It won't be the last."

She paused, as if to give her brother a chance to ask questions. When he didn't, she said, "After Vernon dies, a war between Bevan and Edmund will ignite within the year."

"What news!" he cried in mock surprise. "I would never have supposed it was possible."

"Don't be tiresome!" she said. "Edmund will not win. Bevan might, but the true beneficiary will be the Mother Metropolitan. The Cathedral will win."

"How?" The notion that the Mother Metropolitan would win a war between Edmund and Bevan was absurd on the face of it.

"How is unimportant. What is, is that you, my self-indulgent brother, must make a choice: fight at Bevan's side against Edmund or cling to the Cathedral skirts for the next few years, five or ten, say."

"One of your house snakes tell you that?"

"Oh, do try to keep up. For your purposes, it makes no difference which option you choose. Bevan will do. The Mother Metropolitan will do. What will not do, is for you to stand apart, to sell to both sides and hope to be left alone to total up the profits. You are not Phelan. Your geography is against you. Poor lamb. Stand apart and you will be ground between them like wheat between mill stones."

She sipped her tea, again permitting him a space in which to ask questions, and again he permitted it to lapse. "You could have had Vlod in the palm of your hand. You could have presented his corpse to Bevan or to the Mother Metropolitan. Rather, you've permitted another to perform that service, or attempt to, which amounts to the same thing, politically."

Seldon felt his mind reel. Had she been lying to him? "Was it you, after all?" he demanded. "Were you Fabron's control?"

"No, not me. I've already told you. Don't be such a dunce!"

"Who, then?"

"The appropriate spies are yours, not mine. What do they tell you?"

"About Fabron, nothing, so far, but stay away from Dagna!"

"Your agents are improving. I sensed no one watching us."

"Stay away from her!"

"Am I not obligated to comfort the grieving, to bring justice and solace to the victim, to befriend the friendless?"

"And to proselytize for the Mother Metropolitan?"

"On behalf of the Goddess, above all else," she said. "You profess belief. What objection could you have?"

It occurred to him to counter with the assertion that Dagna was already deeply religious and in no need of proselytizing, that Xenia's main purpose was not religious, but was in fact to enroll Dagna in the clandestine service of the Mother Metropolitan. But such a tactic would have led them out onto old, old ground, into an argument over the difference between belief in the Goddess and devotion to the cult of the Cathedral Henge, which was to say, devotion to the cult of the Mother Metropolitan. He chose to leave that diversion to one side and to strike directly at the center.

"You will not hand over Dagna to the Mother Metropolitan. You will leave Dagna alone."

"Why? For what purpose am I to leave her alone? Am I to leave her alone in order for them to breed her like a farm animal?"

"Spare yourself the exercise. Each of us is bred, our marriages planned, our copulations approved, and our babies judged at birth."

"Have you thought who the next lucky stallion is to be?"

"Jealous?"

Springing to her feet, she struck at him, but he caught her arm by the wrist, stopping the blow as opposed to blocking or turning it. His choice of technique declared his contempt for her attack, for her comparative lack of physical strength.

She threw her weight onto her arm, pressing it toward him, her fingers hooked into talons, but his grip held, and her hand did not move closer to his face.

"Make no mistake," he said, "no, not one! Edmund would happily kill anyone who came between Dagna and her duty to her House. He would kill Dagna herself if she were to betray him." Standing and in the same movement straightening his arm, Seldon pushed his sister back down into her chair. "Stay away from her!"

Regaining her outward calm, Xenia said, "Am I expected to huddle at your feet and tearfully repent and swear my obedience to your commands?"

"I am the head of our house, and I am the head of our clan. You belong to both, and as such, you are obliged to obey me. Your life, like Dagna's and like mine, is to be tendered in the service of our houses."

"I am not one of your—"

He waved her to silence. "Before you vomit out your objections, recall to mind, my dear sister, that I am the Chosen of the Generations of our house. They have anointed me to lead it. Their will and my will are united: we are one in purpose. The Generations act as plenipotentiaries of the Goddess. Therefore, if you'll remember your dogmatics, obedience to me is obedience to the Generations, and obedience to the Generations is obedience to the Goddess. You cannot defy me without defying the Gods and the Generations."

"Handy for you."

"Your sarcasm is beside the point," Seldon said. "Between me and the Henge, there can be no essential conflict. Both are instituted, guided, and tended by the Goddess, and both are unified, brought together without annihilation, by the Harmony, which She both created and chooses to obey, and without which there could be neither life, nor manor, nor Henge."

"You actually believe that tripe! How rustic of you!"

Seldon looked at his sister, studying her. By accident of anger and purpose, he had struck home. He searched, and summoned to himself from inside himself a man whom he had assumed had died, had fled, had turned coward, a man whom he had abandoned. The man he summoned, whom he called, was the chieftain, the war leader, the marshal of armies, the champion of a warrior people. He was the warrior. The man answered his call, and came to him. The man rose up from within him, occupying him as does an unknown strength in the midst of a battle.

His voice deathly quiet, Seldon said, "Dagna is not one of your pets. Leave her alone!"

At the end of a silence, Xenia said, "As you wish, Seldon. I'll not seduce her."

When she had made her good-nights and her hand was on the latch to leave his study, he said, "I do have a third alternative."

"Which is?"

"My own. The one I build for myself."

"You? Fight a war on your own behalf? And win? Don't make me laugh. Narmer would have you for crocodile food." Laughing, she pulled open the door and went out.

A guard closed it behind her, but her laughter penetrated the heavy, metal-bound planks, deriding him as sharply as if she had remained in the room. The sound of it faded as she disappeared down the passage.

His tea was cold, and the pot on the hearth was empty. Had she set a trap, or had she merely tired of toying with him? No, she never tired of baiting him, of goading him to the limits of his endurance.

Before morning, her seamstresses would be hard at work ripping out, re-cutting, and re-stitching the bodices of every piece of clothing she possessed.

She *had* set a trap, but in permitting her to bait him toward it, he had gained the information that he needed to decipher it and to turn it against her.

He sent for three of his favorites, and while he waited for them, he pondered what he had learned from his sister, reworking the information into a series of ordered, useful statements.

By the time the three women, each of them half his age or less, were tapping at his door and cooing their pet names for him, he had his answers. He had his answers solidly in his grasp, and, exactly as he had surmised, and exactly as he had told her, he was his own best alternative!

As for Narmer, Narmer was a cypher.

TWENTY

The closing the of hall's ceremonial doors behind Seldon, his wife, and his sister ended the banquet, and with its ending, a sense of relief filled Vlod. He could not say why, but judging from the expressions on the faces of the people around him, he was not alone.

Although Edmund had stayed on at the head table, to the members of Seldon's court, his presence was of a different order. He was not the manor holder. He was not the chieftain upon whom they relied for their livings. He was a guest in the hall as much as they were, and because he was a fellow guest and not their overlord, they were relaxed in his presence.

Nor was Edmund immune. He was no longer on display, no longer under Seldon's scrutiny. Edmund slouched in his chair with greater ease, drank with greater enjoyment, and laughed with greater volume.

Thanks to the protocols of Seldon's court, it was not yet possible for any of them to leave without giving offense. The manor's hospitality, provided to them through Seldon's generosity, had to be savored for another few minutes. Twenty or thirty would serve to announce to the assembly and to Seldon that his hospitality was appreciated for itself and not for the company of its provider.

While this obeisance to Seldon's honor and to the integrity of his court was being observed, Vlod sipped a glass of wine and pondered the wider social habits of Seldon's clan.

The protocols of the Manor Island were instructive, not that Vlod required lessons in polite behavior.

Instead, the instruction he received was in the emotional timbre that Seldon's protocols engendered among his people, and in what that timbre revealed about day-to-day life on his lands, and in what the proclivities of that life counseled regarding Seldon as a ruler and as a human being.

The lessons were sparse but direct. They were cruel in their power to reveal the private life of his manor. He was not loved, but neither was he feared. He was not hated, but neither did his people view him with indifference or neutrality. He was *liked*. Toward him was shown the deference and affection that might be shown to an employer of middling acumen, fairness, and generosity.

The second lesson was that a second power occupied Seldon's court: Xenia. His people, the whole of Clan Sauvie, were as transparent and as convinced about Xenia as they were opaque and vague about him. She was loved and she was hated, in similar proportions, often by the same groups and classes of people, often by the same person. About her, no indifference was to be discovered.

The third and crucial lesson was also about Xenia. Unlike her brother, she held within her scope the power to ignite and to win a civil war. Her brother could lead his armies against an outside enemy, while Xenia could raise an army of her own and lead its members against Seldon and against their own families.

Xenia had the stomach for such fratricidal butchery, but Seldon did not, and he was the weaker for it. Xenia had the singleness of will to set them to it, and she had the strength and emotional stamina to lead the charge while they slaughtered in her name. They wouldn't notice what they had done until her brother's head was raised on the point of a sword and they were gagging on the smoke from the disposal fires.

Later on, when they had sobered up, if they dared to question her in the slightest, she would hand them reasons and causes for the murder they had done in her name, at her command, and they would willingly believe her and they would love her for it, while the bodies burned and smoke hung thick. When it had cleared, when they had worked into their new lives, they would revere and worship her for what she had done.

Why would they believe her?

In part, because to disbelieve her would be to condemn themselves for being the savages that they had asked her to make of them, and in part, because what she would tell them would be the truth.

Which left a final question. To what end would they slaughter in her name? What would be the result of her ascendancy?

Vlod mulled and he pondered, but no answer introduced itself.

Perhaps he was too exhausted to untangle such a complexity.

He politely put the questions away. He had held himself apart, using the aftermath of his duel with Fabron as a cover for his social selfishness, his misanthropy, and for his curiosity. And, admittedly, he was weary of being alone with his mental ramblings.

When Tremayne's conversation with Brenna reached a pause, Vlod said, "Tre, the negotiations are scheduled to resume the day after tomorrow. Will you be joining Seldon's people?"

Tremayne laughed, and leaning in close, he said, "They wouldn't let me within a hundred klicks." Straightening up, he asked, "Why?"

"I want to talk to you in private before the sessions resume."

"About what?"

"Auguries and spirit journeys. Mine. They've been going sour. I want your opinion."

"Why don't you come by tomorrow?"

"Today, you mean," Vlod said. "I can't. I'm supposed to be sharpening our proposals today."

"It won't take you the whole day, will it? Every year Edmund presents the same proposal. He drags out his dredging costs, bellows about Seldon's prices, and promptly cuts Seldon's balls off, financially speaking. Next comes Seldon's turn. He yells like a castrated pig about the increased transit fees, and weeps for days about the strangulation of commerce."

"That's about where they left things the day before yesterday."

"I thought as much. Tomorrow, Edmund will reopen negotiations by moderating his demands, and in a couple of days, Seldon will dry his eyes, sign at the bottom of the page, and then, in the middle of the winter, when trade is at a premium, he'll raise his prices. What's the point, except bloated treasuries?"

"How much experience do you have at operating deep-water dredges?" Brenna asked.

"How many silk farms have you operated?" Tremayne asked.

"We aren't allowed access to silkworms, by treaty."

"We aren't allowed access to deep water, by treaty."

A fire kindled in Brenna's eyes. "A treaty is nothing but smears of ink on paper."

"Then why don't you come and take the silk?" Tremayne asked.

"Why don't you come and break out into deep water?"

Defusing the exchange, Vlod said, "Because we're both too busy raising our prices."

"True," Tremayne said, pitching the word in a manner that broke the tension between the three of them. "The part that bewilders me is that Seldon is getting richer every year." After a space, he asked, "Is Edmund losing money on his transit fees? Does he collect less than it costs him to keep the channels open?"

"Tre! I can't tell you that."

"Or won't. Sorry. I keep forgetting who we have to be."

By this time, a significant number of the men and women of Seldon's court had left the hall, and Edmund's people were now openly drifting away.

Vlod made a sweeping gesture toward the center of the room. "We'll be the last ones out unless we hurry."

"Father left a while ago," Brenna commented.

Tremayne finished his drink. "About your augury," he began. His tone expressed his confidence in Vlod and offered his reassurances and his discretion, but it fell wrong despite his efforts. "Let's go up to my rooms and talk about it."

"To hell with sleep?" Vlod asked.

"To hell with the loss of a perfectly good night," Tremayne said.

The way to Tremayne's rooms led them along one of the quays.

The wharves and special-purpose foundries were a chaos of activity, but farther out, beyond the ships and barges tied up alongside, the inner harbor was unimaginably calm. The anchored vessels lay as though cradled in a deep slumber.

The quay merged into a sea wall, complete with an ornate promenade. The promenade was stepped off with benches, and at intervals, ramps led down to floating docks that were used by the manor's larger pleasure craft.

Pointing at a thirty-oared cruiser, Tremayne said, "Seldon's latest. He did a lot of the work on her himself."

"Pretty," Brenna said.

"With three to an oar, she's fast, too," Tremayne said.

The craft had high, flared bows, a heavily built stem that curved down into a generous ram with which to defend herself, an abundance of freeboard for a river vessel, a noticeably small porthole fitted in the aft cabin, and large, elongated scuppers.

The feature that interested Vlod the most was the cruiser's rig. Her two masts were short and thick in comparison to the normal run of river galleys, and her booms and yards were proportionally short and heavy. The boat's standing and running rigging were at least two sizes larger than one would expect to find on any vessel of a similar size built for inland waters. The sails that would be fit to those booms and yards would be small in relationship to the overall size and weight of the vessel and to the size of her crew, assuming that she was to be used on the Columbia.

"What's the draft?" Vlod asked, with as much idle curiosity as he could muster.

Tremayne gave him a disparaging look. "Whom do you think you're kidding?" he asked. "She draws one and two-thirds meters, and carries lots of ballast in the form of iron ingots. Cedar on steam-bent oak, teak decks, five frames to the meter, bronze fastenings, hemp cordage, a balanced rudder as big as the Great Gate of Shillapoo, chain pumps fore and aft, and copper-bottomed."

"A sea boat."

"Let's say she's overbuilt to go picnicking on your favorite island."

"Seldon would wet his pants in deep water," Brenna said.

"Be that as it may," Tremayne said, moving on, "he's built himself a deep-water yacht."

Walking fast in order to keep up with him, Vlod asked, "What will he do with her?"

"Pay the transit fees and go yachting on the ocean, I guess. He doesn't confide in me."

They reached the end of the promenade. Directly ahead of them was the garden wall of the manor's henge.

To their right was a service street that led up into one of the commercial districts.

To their left was the Western Colonnade, one of the four colonnades that led out onto the Pool of Eileen.

Each of the colonnades was built of white marble and was oriented to one of the cardinal compass points. Where they met, in the exact center of the Pool, they joined in the sacrificial temple that bore Eileen's name.

The Temple of Eileen was dedicated to the Goddess; however, it also memorialized Eileen and enshrined the oldest continuously active site of the Goddess's sacrificial worship in the Columbia River Basin.

Constructed of white and pink marble with black, red, and gold accents, the Temple of Eileen was arguably the most beautiful structure in the whole of the basin. Surrounded by the night-blackened waters of the Pool, the central complex appeared to float, not in the water but above it. It appeared to have been offered up into the moonlight by the four colonnades.

Strikingly, in that same moonlight, the whole of the complex glowed as though each marble block, each delicately carved arch, each tile and fitting, each ornate screen, were lit from within.

Architecturally, the temple was a low, octagonal structure, topped by a tall central spire. Its layered roofs and side galleries, its colonnades and spire made it appear light, ethereal, and at the same time, rooted in the earth, in the water of the Pool, in the eternal essence of the earth, in the everlasting waters of life and death.

As a building, as a material object, it presented a riddle. It was solid, substantial, unmoving. Its builders had driven its foundations deep into the ground beneath the bottom of the Pool. Those foundations were rooted and unyielding, and yet, the Temple was also delicate; it was a fragile tracery in stone, a mirage in marble that hovered above the Pool's moonlit water.

Tremayne stepped out onto the nearest colonnade. Waving for them to follow him, he said, "Shortcut. It's either this or go up into town and circle around in front of the henge."

The southern colonnade connected the Pool to the manor henge. The henge was older, vastly larger, and far less intriguing than the Temple of Eileen. The walls of the residence and administrative buildings had watch towers at their corners, and were, predictably, crenelated in between. Taken as a whole, their walls were like slabs of bleak, gray stone that glowered down upon the outside world.

"Come on!" Tremayne said. "It's getting late."

They followed.

Vlod had no reason to believe that walking through the colonnade for other than religious purposes was forbidden, and yet he was aware, or suspected that he was aware, of a dozen pairs of eyes watching them, watching and disapproving.

Instead of going around the Temple of Eileen and continuing on across the Pool via the Eastern Colonnade, Tremayne entered the Temple.

Vlod and Brenna followed him.

Vlod had seen the Temple many times before from the outside, had heard or read many of its stories and legends, but, incredibly, he had never gone inside before. As he passed under the lintel above the doorway connecting the colonnade and the Temple, as he stepped across the threshold, he experienced what he could only explain to himself as the Temple's history pressing in upon him, pressing in and pushing him back, seeking to drive him away.

The doorway opened into a series of switchbacks and mazes, the Wheel of Awakening. Through its structure, through the experience of transiting it, the Wheel instructed and intrigued, it surprised and delighted, it did not frighten or deter or dominate. The walls were blank, the floors worn by centuries of feet.

The Wheel opened into the heart of the Temple. This central chamber was larger and taller than Vlod had anticipated. It was circular, with sides that curved upwards towards one another but at a good height that made a reverse turn and continued gracefully on up through a band of arched windows into the core of the spire, which soared above the building.

At intervals along the walls, brass oil lamps lit the interior.

The sound of their boots on the pavement echoed.

The floor of the chamber descended in a series of concentric rings to the edge of a pool of clear water. On the north side, an elevated platform extended out over the pool.

Vlod's stomach lurched, and he realized that he was looking at the Temple's sacrificial pool.

The surface of the water was smooth and motionless, as clear as a sharp day in winter.

The bottom of the pool was lost to view in its blue-black depths, lost beyond the reach of the pale light of the oil lamps.

"Have I shown you around before?" Tremayne asked.

"No," Vlod said, and hoped that sooner or later, his feeling of trespass would dissipate.

Tremayne said, "No one can say how deep the pool is, but the first fifty meters were lined with glazed tile when the temple was built. As for the water itself, it isn't river seepage like most of the other wells on the island. It's spring water." He grinned. "I've tested it."

Vlod felt a sinking sensation at the thought of the risks Tremayne must have taken to satisfy his curiosity.

Tremayne climbed down the rings to the edge of the pool and trailed his fingers in the water. "The Tears of Eileen," he said. "In days gone by, the priestesses are supposed to have salted the water. For a while, a couple of centuries ago, they were claiming cures on its behalf and selling it by the bottle. Very lucrative according to what I've read."

"Are we in for another one of your lectures?" Brenna asked.

"Naturally. You might learn something," Tremayne said. "After a few years, the trade turned commercial in the worst sense. To their credit, the priestesses understood what was happening, and put a halt to it. They stopped their own trade."

"Unusual," Brenna said. She glanced around the chamber. "There is a sense of the spiritual here, though."

"Spirituality and centuries of indiscriminate death," Tremayne said. "Ramsey's Rule was born here. He put his signature to it and read it out right over there on the platform."

"I'm fairly vague on Ramsey's details," Vlod said.

Climbing up from the edge of the pool, Tremayne went on, his voice distant, as though he were lecturing to an unseen audience or guiding a tour through his museum. "At the close of the so-called Second Reawakening, Ramsey the Warlord, not Ramsey the Money Striker, persuaded the priestesses to offer just one victim to the Goddess just once every year. Ramsey's Rule: one in one. He further stipulated that the victim had to be one of the cult's priestesses or priests, and not someone chosen at whim from among the cult's followers. He reasoned that if the priestesses or priests were willing to worship the Goddess in the manner they had adopted, then they ought to be willing to die for Her themselves as well as be willing to kill for Her. It was a masterful reform. It restored a measure of sanity to the society of his day."

"How so?" Brenna asked. "Most cults offer human sacrifices."

"By the hundreds?" Tremayne asked. "What's left out of the histories and legends and stories of the period is that the Second Reawakening was an era of social and religious psychosis. The triggering event had been lost in the babble of argument that flowed among the contemporary chroniclers of that age. Often the rulers in power burned, altered, or falsified the records, either at the time the chroniclers were setting them down or not long after. Anyone who complained was dealt with summarily. Therefore, the records available are, as they say in Thaddeus' circle, 'historically accurate but not pedantically precise.'"

"'Truths told with lies,'" Vlod said, intoning part of an old Academy aphorism.

"Be that as it may," Tremayne said, "whatever the cause, the hysteria raged unchecked throughout the basin for most of two generations. In the end, Ramsey the Warlord put his sword to their throats and forced sanity upon them. Once he'd taken action, the surrounding manor holders and chieftains followed in his footsteps, and the one-victim rule was adopted."

"How did Ramsey break loose?" Vlod asked. "Or had he kept himself apart?"

"No, not him! He was just as caught up in the death and ecstasy as anyone, but the downward spiral of his economic and census figures gradually shocked him into a sobering awareness of what was happening. His people were suffering from self-inflicted genocide."

Tremayne walked out onto the platform. "They brought them here. The priestesses weighted them down with gold in the beginning, then lead, then iron, and at the height of the hysteria, with sacks of rock. Flower garlands were put around their heads." Making a two-handed shoving motion, he finished, "And off they went, down into the cool, clear, unknown depths of the Pool of Eileen. As a kindness, before pushing them in, they'd stab the ones who were terrified of drowning, but they were always scrupulous to ensure that the victims died in the pool and not on the platform."

Vlod felt disgusted with himself for respecting Eileen, which he did. It was unfair to blame her for the horrors committed by those who followed her. But the pool bore her name, and she had founded the cult built around it. She had set it in motion, and she had forged its purposes. The responsibility was hers.

"Time to go," Tremayne said.

"Not a moment too soon," Brenna said.

"What's amiss?" Vlod asked.

"We have company," she said, and loosened the draw catch on her battle knife.

As Vlod and the others stepped onto the eastern colonnade, a black-robed figure stepped out of the shadows and stood, impassively in plain view, watching them leave.

"Eileen's ghost," Tremayne commented, and strode on towards the shore.

As curator of the Holbrook Museum, Tremayne was quartered on its uppermost floor.

Holbrook the Pious had sited his museum such that an obsolete, hexagonal blockhouse formed its southwest corner, the corner farthest from the main entrance. The back entrance, the one Tremayne habitually used, opened into the blockhouse.

As they reached its foot, the moon was lowering behind the inner curtain wall.

Vlod felt as though he were approaching a place of dark, half-seen truths, a place where nightmare overpowered the waking world. After the Temple of Eileen, such an emotion, such an intuition, was only to be expected.

Tremayne produced one key and drew back the siege bolts. He produced another and opened the door.

When they were inside, he relocked the door, and using an iron level, re-engaged the siege bolts. Their locking mechanism made a loud *click*.

Using a steel and flint, Tremayne lit a handheld lamp. When he had it burning steadily and the wick adjusted, he led them up into the block-house, level after level.

The stairs were devoid of railings. They spiraled around to the left, and kept to the outside wall for the first three layers, which were equipped with storage floors in the center.

Vlod envied Tremayne his tower. The envy was genuine, but it was also hollow, mitigated.

Towers like Tremayne's came with chieftain's like Tremayne's.

Not a pretty thought.

At the very top of the stairs, Tremayne unlocked and led them into the sitting room of his apartment.

They opted for tea, and Tremayne made it.

They sat around a low, circular table, one littered with papers, dishes, and mugs. Some had mold floating on their remaining contents.

The room smelled of cooking, laundry waiting in a wicker basket, recently worked teak, pine shavings, and of smoke.

Setting his mug on the table, Tremayne asked, "About your auguries, what happened?"

Vlod said, "I used—"

Brenna stopped him. "Sorry to spoil your fun, but I'd rather we didn't discuss Vlod's auguries here."

"Vlod?" Tremayne asked.

"I serve her father's House," Vlod said. "Tomorrow aboard *Koan*?"

"Fine," Brenna said, "but not here and not tonight."

"It's your choice," Tremayne said.

"Indeed, it is," Brenna said.

Changing subjects, Tremayne said, "Here, let me show you my latest." He set a large object in the middle of the table and pulled off the covering. It was the partially completed bust of a young woman, carefully carved in teak. "I built up the rough block from the scraps from Seldon's yacht. Notice the effect. I had no idea that using a laminate would turn out as well as it has."

The woman was beautiful. She had gentle features and a gentle expression. But she possessed strength, too, beneath her benign, beguiling surface.

Teak was an appropriate wood for such a face, and the fact that the bust was carved from a block made up of many pieces, said something instructive about its subject.

"Who is she?" Vlod asked.

"Lyrisette," Tremayne said. "She was one of Xenia's dancers."

"Are you in love with her?" Brenna asked. "One of Xenia's dancers would be a dangerous person to fall in love with."

"I don't remember seeing her tonight," Vlod said. "Was she at the banquet?"

"She was not," Tremayne said. "Xenia sent her back to the Cathedral."

"She'll be all right, won't she?" Brenna asked.

"I'd rather she were here," Tremayne said, "for her sake as well as mine."

Promising a shortcut, Tremayne offered to walk them back to the hall, and they accepted. Despite what he'd said, Vlod wasn't entirely ready to give up on getting Tremayne's opinion about the auguries.

They were skirting the Pool of Eileen when a long figure entered the perimeter street from the northern causeway. The man was clothed in black, and moved with slow deliberation, as though he wanted to be observed.

"Another of Eileen's ghosts?" Vlod asked.

"Fabron's."

"Then you'd better turn back."

"And miss the fun?"

"You'll be in the way," Vlod said.

"You little bastard!" Tremayne said, partly in mock indignation and part in genuine anger.

"I'm sorry, Tre; I put that badly. I meant to say that if it is one of Fabron's then I want him to attack, and he might not if you're with us." Vlod embraced his friend in parting. "Come by tomorrow."

Standing back, Tremayne smiled. "Wouldn't miss it."

It was half past four in the morning, and the air was sharp with cold. They were nearing the hall, and there ought to have been people about, but the streets were dark and empty.

They entered the hall's rear courtyard, and started across it toward the kitchen entrance. The yard was deserted, and for the moment, the watch's rounds had taken them elsewhere.

A torch fluttered in a gust of wind that had wandered in from the river. The puff of air smelled of the burning pitch from the torch and—

Vlod reached to edge Brenna away from him, but his thrust met with empty space. He followed his arm, and rolled onto the ground, coming out in a low, wide crouch. Brenna leapt forward, also rolling, distancing herself from Vlod, and was just rising into a similar stance, her battle knife drawn. She was facing back along the route they had taken.

Brenna in the torchlight, the black paving stones and the shuttered windows, the doorways. The planes and angles of the shadows along the street, the glint of steel. An unseen but mortal enemy.

Vlod's sword, the Matsuri blade, sang from its scabbard!

Twenty-One

The echoes of the blade's song mingled with the odors of old cooking grease, spilled wine, and dirty sweat. The overlays were subtle but noisome in the air.

Although their route had brought them back to the hall through an open courtyard outside the kitchens, these filthy, septic odors were out of place.

Brenna dodged to the right.

A throwing knife struck the paving stones and slid away into the shadows.

A second knife flashed in the torchlight as it arced toward her, but at the last moment, she pivoted and blocked the knife with her forearm, sending it cartwheeling.

Seemingly of its own, Brenna's battle knife flew into an unlighted space between two wagons that were standing a few meters to one side of the kitchen doors.

A scream filled the courtyard, and a black-cloaked figured staggered out into the torchlight. It pitched forward onto the paving stones, groaned, and died.

"Vlod!"

It was Brenna's voice.

Vlod understood the warning and heard the boot-falls in the same instant. He wheeled around.

The steel of his sword caught the torchlight and held it. The weapon glowed as though it were alive.

Vlod took his assailant's downward stroke on the blade's forte, and slipped away to the side, releasing his attacker's blade, a standard combat sword.

It was the sort of weapon that a man-at-arms would take into a land or naval battle but that only an over-proud dolt would carry into an assassin's ambush.

The sword clanged against a pavement, and the man wielding it grunted with the exertion of trying to regain his balance. His efforts, however, were too unskilled and too late. He stumbled forward, and Vlod used his knee to strike him in the back and flatten him onto the pavement.

The man scrambled to his feet and renewed his attack, but Vlod stepped adroitly to one side, parrying with his own weapon. The man carried on beyond him, a charging bull, head down.

Brenna was waiting for him.

He swung at her with his sword in an overheard arc, but she, too, dodged and counterattacked through the resulting opening. She kicked low and hard, driving her foot solidly into his gut.

He emitted an enormous "Whoopf!" and stumbled away from her.

To no avail.

In a whirling series of kicks and strikes, she narrowed the fighting distance between them. She moved inside his guard.

He struggled to bring his sword into use, to lengthen the distance between them, but before he could manage it, she opened his throat with her hideout knife.

The would-be assassin dropped to the ground and thrashed from side to side, clutching at his throat. He couldn't scream. He could only make frantic bubbling sounds as his blood splashed out onto the ground, like water from an upended jug.

An arrow whined into the courtyard from the wall above them.

Brenna cried in sudden pain. The arrow had slashed her leg, opening a deep, bloody cut.

"They could at least shoot straight," she said.

No sooner had the quip left her mouth than her leg collapsed out from under her, and she ended up sprawled on the pavement.

"Son of a bitch!" she swore through clenched teeth, and flattened herself in the scant protection offered by the body of the man she had just killed.

She found his battle knife and drew it. Two knives, and how many would-be assassins were left?

She ought to have worn a sword. Protocol be damned!

Vlod ran into the open, hoping to draw the archer's fire away from Brenna.

The ploy worked, for when a second arrow whined into the courtyard, it struck between Vlod's feet.

He feinted to his left, then switching directions, he swung around, spinning as a dancer spins but with a far deadlier intent.

Perched on the top of a wall, the archer was a shadow against the sky, an irregular shape not far from a smoking chimney.

Movement: he was drawing a third arrow from his quiver.

In rapid succession, Vlod drew his battle knife and his backup and threw each up toward the archer.

One missed, but the other struck, making a dull thud.

At first, the archer stood motionless, but after a second or two he stiffened, his weight shifted, and he fell, screaming. He landed in a pile on the paving stones.

"One left," Brenna called, her voice rippling along the buildings facing the courtyard.

Windows opened, and faces appeared. Seldon's servants stared, chattering and calling to one another. Someone was yelling for the guard.

Vlod crossed over to Brenna and examined her leg, pulling away the compress she had improvised. Blood was flowing and pumping and a fairly decent sized puddle had formed under her. The arrow had severed one of the minor arteries in her leg. It had also done its fair share of tissue damage.

"We have an audience," Vlod said, and pulled the belt from his tunic.

"Naturally. The incompetent who's trying to kill you can't do anything right." She winced as he tied the belt around her leg above the arrow wound. "His men can't shoot straight and he can't work an ambush worth shit."

"I guess I need to attract a better class of enemy."

Vlod pushed the scabbarded blade of his battle knife into the knot in his belt.

"You'd better or your reputation is going to suffer."

He twisted the knot, tightening the tourniquet.

"I better get you inside," Vlod said.

Levering herself upright, Brenna said, "Go to hell!" Her face white with pain, she pushed herself farther up into a crouch. Bracing herself, she said, "Go ahead! Call out the fucking bastard!"

"Don't blame me if you bleed out."

"Not likely."

Taking his sword in hand, Vlod stood and moved a pace or two away from her.

He switched his sword from hand to hand, idly limbering his wrist, and looked into the doorways and ground-level windows.

He went on to the dark patches behind and under the carriages and wagons, and then on to the gray-black places next to the few shrubs that Seldon had permitted in the courtyard.

Vlod found nothing, but he knew who was there, the leader of this little fiasco, hiding, waiting, hoping, but afraid to strike openly.

"Fabron! Show yourself!"

The sound of Vlod's voice rolled along the stone walls like the peel of an avenging thunder.

"Fabron! I am here. I await your pleasure."

Silence.

"It is time we finished it."

Tremayne entered the courtyard through one of the nearer gateways and started toward Vlod.

"Stay where you are, my friend," Vlod said. "This affair is of the clan and the house I serve!"

Tremayne stopped in his tracks.

A foot, somewhere close to the courtyard's harbor-side exit, brushed across the cobbles.

"Fabron! Was your courage spawned in a cesspit?"

Brenna muttered, "Some insult! I'll have to teach you."

"I agree," Tremayne said. "The quality of your insult is, in and of itself, insulting." Using the words as a distraction, Tremayne came forward.

"Cover Brenna," Vlod said.

"As you wish," the older magus said.

A foot crunched on a scattering of loose gravel, and a throwing knife whistled from the area by the gate that led out of the courtyard on the harbor side.

Vlod flicked the knife from the air with the tip of his small sword.

"I've had enough of knives. Let us have done!"

After an extended silence, one that betrayed his reluctance and his compulsion, Fabron stepped into the light, and drew his rapier. He had nothing left to do but to see his attack through to its end.

Vlod adjusted his stance, and waited for the larger, heavier man to close the distance between them.

Fabron's stride, the manner of the way his feet moved, announced his fatigue and his fear of facing the magus.

Without technical display or ostentation, he drew his guarding dagger and came on guard. "The night is ours," he said. "Let us make of it what we will!"

It was a pretty speech, but his heart wasn't in it. He was walking to a gallows of his own making. Who, Vlod wondered, had given him the wood, the nails, the hinges, and the rope?

Vlod had his guesses, but those would have to wait for hard evidence.

The silence in the courtyard grew into a presence as real as the anticipation of dawn that was being written in the eastern sky and as real and as superficial as the curiosity of Seldon's servants.

Smoke drifted out from the kitchens through the opened doors and windows, doors and windows that were crowded with people.

Nor was this the extent of the curious. Scores of people had come to the windows of their apartments or had pressed themselves into the gateways and doorways of the residence wing of the hall.

They had come with a single purpose: to watch the final confrontation, to see a violent death.

It went beyond idle curiosity or simple bloodlust, this interest of theirs. A member of their chieftain's court had insulted the honor of the magus of one of their chieftain's allies, and now the debt created by that insult was to be discharged.

They had known at the banquet that Fabron's defeat, as though in a respectful fencing match, that his minimal humiliation at the magus's hands, had not restored the ruptured Harmony.

"How could it?" they whispered among themselves.

Fabron had run up the bill deliberately, and tonight he had made matters worse. He had attempted to ambush Vlod and Brenna. Fabron's actions and his methods were wrong, he had besmirched the hospitality of Seldon's court, and if Vlod did not take Fabron's life, then they offered the opinion that their chieftain would have no choice but to do it, if only to show that he was their chieftain.

But over and above such considerations, what drew them, what held them was a question: why had Fabron risked so much for the transient and questionable pleasure of insulting a magus?

When it came, Fabron's attack took the form of a single lunge. No warning, no fencing, no testing—strong and brilliant—a lunge toward the inside, straight and powerful. It was a dueling technique that required inordinate skill. It was an attack that was utterly unexpected from a man of Fabron's caliber.

Vlod parried with his dagger and riposted.

Fabron parried.

Striking inside the parry, Vlod reversed his stance, left foot brought forward, and slapped the side of his blade on Fabron's forearm, hard.

Fabron's rapier fell from his hand, and he yelled in pain, striking out with his dagger, protecting himself with a counterattack.

Vlod blocked, and reversed himself a second time.

He advanced, and taking Fabron's dagger with his own, he lunged, directing his blade very low, thereby avoiding a mortal stroke. His small sword bit into Fabron's leg just above the knee. The tip of the blade scraped along the man's bone. Fabron bellowed in pain and dropped to the ground as Vlod withdrew his sword. Blood spurted from the puncture wound.

Leg for leg, it seemed only fair.

Fabron's eyes were oversized with terror, but he was not yet so far gone as to no longer be a threat. His hand worked on his dagger, trying for a throwing hold.

Vlod brought his foot down, crushing the hand between his boot and the paving stones. The sounds of grinding cartilage and snapping bone whispered into the night air.

Vlod pressed the point of his blade into the underside of Fabron's chin, and once he was sure that Fabron understood his situation, Vlod asked, "Who sent you?"

"They'll kill my family."

"They?" Vlod worked the blade enough, he judged coldly, to cause a burst of pain. "Who are *they*?"

"Tell my wife that I love her."

Vlod made to pull his blade away from the man's throat, but he acted a fraction of a second too late. By the time he realized what was happening, Fabron had pushed down with his chin and had simultaneously thrown himself up and forward, forcing the point through and out the back of his neck. He twisted to one side, completing the cut.

Vlod pulled his sword away, but there was nothing to be done but watch the blood spurt from Fabron's neck.

When Fabron was finally dead, Vlod closed the man's eyes.

Would those who'd sent him set aside the effort once and for all, or would they try again?

He hoped that they would make peace with his existence, that they would accept that enough blood and had been poured out onto the ground, but Vlod also recognized that such a hope was the deadliest sort of fantasy.

In the meantime, before their next attack fell, Vlod had Brenna's wound to attend to. Like as not, it would require stitches.

Brenna hated stitches.

Turn the page for a preview chapter of the next book in The Assassins of Harmony series, *The Return of the Vision Dancer.*

ONE

Within a quarter of an hour after Fabron's unsuccessful attack outside Seldon's Hall, Vlod was tucked away in Edmund's suite of rooms, plying his skills as a combat medic. The immediate task was to wash out Brenna's arrow wound, gently scrubbing and irrigating with water that was as clean as possible.

Finishing, he handed the blood-stained cloth to a waiting man-at-arms. The gash in Brenna's thigh was continuing to bleed, but the rate had slowed.

Good. Her body was making an effort to care for itself.

Still, being no fan of blood loss, Vlod tightened the tourniquet around her upper thigh. The tourniquet was a proper leather strap, one that he had exchanged for his belt.

Brenna sucked in a sharp breath, but the trickle of fresh blood stopped. Her leg below the tourniquet was white, while that above was unnaturally red.

"I'll loosen it as soon as I'm through," Vlod said.

"Get on with it." Brenna's voice was strong but tinged with the unmistakable signs of shock.

Vlod opened a glass bottle of double-distilled alcohol and held it poised above the opening. "Disinfectant. It'll sting."

"You're a damned liar," Brenna said.

Vlod was going to be sick. His hands were frozen in place, except that they were trembling. He'd treated dozens of cuts, gashes, and punctures, most of them much worse. None of those had bothered him as much as Brenna's wound was.

He'd had the odd attack of queasiness: compound fractures did that to him, and belly wounds; but compound fractures and belly wounds did that to everyone, so he could dismiss his innate sensitivity as a factor.

He pulled his hands back away from her.

Edmund, Wolfram, and Tremayne were watching him, and Brenna was waiting for him to finish.

It was up to him. No one else was going to complete the dressing. She wouldn't allow them to, and Vlod wasn't about to stand aside, not even for Tremayne.

Vlod's problem was that he was treating Brenna, and because he was, he was unable to blot out his understanding of the pain he was causing her, his understanding of the wretched horror that might lay ahead of her if he were practicing incompetently: gangrene, amputation, fever, delirium, a slow death as the infection ate through her, as it killed her while leaving him to live the rest of his life to without her.

He attempted to enter into one mantra after another, but abandoned each of his attempts. His mind was welded to her, and hammer at the join as he would, he could not break it loose.

The seconds raced by, and then without his understanding why, Brenna herself became his mantra, and his fears receded. His love for her turned strict, demanding, and brutal, but it was no less intense, no less love.

He dribbled a stream of the clear liquid into and around the opening, but the effect was closer to spilling than applying, and a large amount of the alcohol ended up soaking the table around her leg. Her muscles twitched, but the leg itself did not move.

She took in a vast gulp of air, and said, "You *are* a damned fucking liar!"

"Thanks. I'm really proud of my lying." He handed the bottle to the man-at-arms, who half-filled a drinking glass with the nearly pure alcohol and handed it to Vlod, who gave it to Brenna. "Here. Cauterize your tonsils."

She drained the glass.

Setting it beside her, she said, "It isn't fair! You're the one who ought to be on my end. After all, they wanted to kill you, not me, and here I am doing your dirty work for you."

"Let's hope not," he said. "I've taken great pains—well, effort—to see to it that there is as little dirt involved as possible. Infection is the warrior's most deadly enemy," he said, voicing the last as though he were a pompous fool delivering what he believed to be the unalloyed wisdom of the ages. "Besides, I've always been a lazy bastard, making other people do the work for me whenever I can."

"One favor. I keep it, right?"

He picked up the needle and thread he'd prepared and held it just above her skin. His nausea broke in a wave. The contents of his stomach surged up into his throat, gagging him. He compelled himself to hold it down and to wait until the spasm let go of him. He'd sewn up hundreds of similar cuts and gashes, many of them worse. Edmund and Wolfram both carried the scars of his workman-like stitchery. Her wound was a whole lot of nothing, and he was determined not to fail her!

"It needs a vertical scar, one running along the leg instead of across it," he said, "but it's going to get a horizontal one, following the line of the cut."

"No signatures?" Wolfram asked.

"I don't have room for one," Vlod said.

"Damn!" Brenna said. "I was looking forward to a fancy scar."

"I can assure you that you won't be disappointed," Vlod said, and pushed the needle down through the layers of skin on one side of the gash and up through the layers of skin on the other. He pulled the thread snug, and tied it off, completing the first stitch.

Brenna gritted her teeth but she did not cry out.

A second glass of the double-distilled followed the first.

Working as carefully and as fast as he could, he closed the wound, leaving the closure tight enough to heal properly but also, he prayed, open enough to drain while it healed. Proper drainage was critical. Without it, the wound would turn septic.

But should he be closing it at all? Was it too deep to close? But if he didn't close it, what was he going to do with it? No, the thing to do was to close it, to close it and be damned sure that it drained and didn't infect.

No infection. So and blessed let it be!

When he had tied off the last knot and set the needle aside, Brenna lay back on the table. Her face was dangerously pale, and her eyes were damp.

He released the tourniquet, and within a couple of minutes, the color had returned to her lower leg and the scant but steady flow of fresh blood from the wound that he had wanted to achieve appeared. The blood would clot, and the wound would heal.

Bandaging her leg, he said, "You keep it."

Her eyes had taken on a distant, glassy look, and the alcohol had long since taken effect. She said, "Next time, you take the arrow. I wouldn't want to be selfish."

"As you wish. Next time, the arrow is mine," Vlod said.

Surprised at how light she was, Vlod carried her to her bed and laid her down. Edmund had already turned back the bedclothes, and now he made his daughter comfortable.

Wolfram and Tremayne waited in one corner or the room.

Brenna caught Vlod's arm. "Will you tell her?"

"Tell whom?

"His wife. Fabron's wife."

"Tremayne will take care of it."

"You ought to go."

"I killed him, remember?"

She nodded her understanding.

Vlod checked the covers without inspecting his chieftain's work and stepped out into the hallway that connected the room to the front of the suite.

Edmund posted a guard, and Wolfram occupied himself by pacing the length of the sitting room. He may as well have been on the galley's quarterdeck.

Edmund sat in a chair and rubbed his forehead with the heels of his hands, as though he were trying to clear his mind. "Where's Dagna?"

"Staying aboard," Wolfram said. "I have her guarded. She's safe."

"Very well," Edmund said. He got up. "I need to have a chat with my brother chieftain," he said, and left the rooms, bellowing for the captain of the guard to double the sentries.

"I'll inform the widow," Tremayne said, and left.

Wolfram's pacing held to its beat. It took him from the north wall of the room across to the south, and from the south wall back across to the north, again and again. His boots struck a determined, defiant rhythm on the floor. After several circuits, the battlemaster said, "Tell me about Fabron."

"Tell you what?"

"He was a suicide."

"I've said that he was."

"How did he do it?"

"I've already told you."

"I want it fresh."

"As you wish," Vlod said. "Fabron pushed himself up onto the point of my sword. It exited through the rear of his neck just below the base of his skull. He acted very fast. I couldn't have prevented it."

"But once he'd started, you figured he was a dead man, so you let him finish."

"I didn't *let* him do anything."

"He caught you off guard?"

"I wasn't expecting him to commit suicide, nor, I believe, was he," Vlod said. "As I said, he was very quick and very determined. He must have made his decision when he realized that I was intent on taking him alive. He couldn't have believed that I was going to turn him loose a second time."

Wolfram completed another circuit. "He was afraid of someone, then. Someone who isn't you or me. By and large, the first thing that people facing torture do, is to convince themselves that they'll find a way to outsmart their captors." Another circuit. "It's their certainty that they'll break under torture that leads them to commit suicide."

"I don't think he was afraid for himself," Vlod said. "He told me that *they* would kill his family."

"Bevan's people?"

"Possibly, but Bevan's hand may not be the hand at work."

"Assume that it is," Wolfram said.

"In that case, I have a question for you: Are you afraid of Bevan? More to the point, would you commit suicide rather than fail him?"

"I'm not Fabron."

"He was no coward, and he wasn't dumb, much less stupid," Vlod said. "He would have swatted Bevan away as easily as you or I would swat away a mosquito. He was afraid of someone, agreed, but he was not afraid of Bevan."

Jamie McNabb writes in several genres, but concentrates on science fiction and fantasy. His work appears in the *Universe Between, Past Crimes, Pulse Pounders, Valor,* and other issues of *Fiction River,* as well as in a variety of online and print publications.

Jamie has sailed extensively on the Columbia and Willamette rivers, where *The Assassins of Harmony* series takes place.

For further information and to subscribe to his newsletter, please visit his website: www.jamicmcnabb.com or go to https://landing.mailerlite.com/webforms/landing/w7k8s7.

THE ASSASSINS OF HARMONY

The Turning of the Wheel

Ulricka's Gambit

The Heretic's Son

The Chosen of the Generations

In Seldon's Hall

The Return of the Vision Dancer

www.ingramcontent.com/pod-product-compliance
Lightning Source LLC
Chambersburg PA
CBHW011224190726
48287CB00008B/2742